No. 8

ANN THORNE—REPORTER

THE CORONET LIBRARY

Smiling and a little shy she stood among her
friends.

(*See page* 110).

ANN THORNE
REPORTER

by

ROSAMOND BERTRAM

Illustrated by
JOHN BENISON

THOMAS NELSON AND SONS LTD
LONDON EDINBURGH PARIS MELBOURNE
TORONTO AND NEW YORK

CONTENTS

LIST OF ILLUSTRATIONS

ANN THORNE—REPORTER

CHAPTER ONE

A BIRTHDAY THRILL

THE moment she woke up that morning Ann thought, " I'm seventeen. I'm grown-up."

It seemed to her a tremendous thing to have passed the barrier between girlhood and adult life. For, to Ann, seventeen was the age when one became a woman—a grown, independent woman, ready to fight the world on its own terms.

" Why," she thought, smiling a little, " my own mother was married at seventeen ! She was only eighteen when I arrived. But I don't want to think of such things as marriage. Work. A career. Success in my chosen job. That's what I'll have somehow; I will, I *will*! My chance will come some time, though I wish it would hurry up."

In the sunshine that poured through her bedroom window she stretched and sat up, sniffing delicately as she identified an odour that stole upstairs. Coffee. Darling Aunt Helen, she always got up early and made breakfast for Ann ! There was no one in all the world like Aunt Helen for kindness and practical sympathy and dependability.

In fact, she would be quite perfect were it not for her tendency to laugh gently at Ann's burning ambition to be a " star " reporter on a great national newspaper.

" Darling, it's an absurd thing to set your heart on," she would say. " Big newspapers don't pick their staffs from little country towns like this. What editor will ever hear of you, and what would you have to offer him ? "

" Everything," Ann would counter stubbornly. " I'm young and I'm getting a fine training here, even if the paper I work for is only a local four-sheet rag. I bet I could make a success on a national paper if only I could get the chance."

" That's just the point. I expect every reporter up and down the country thinks he or she could be a shining light in Fleet Street if only the chance came along. But such chances *don't* come along. No, no, my dear. You carry on with your job here for a few more years, and then you'll get married and settle down and forget these notions."

The tears would press behind Ann's eyes, and she would fall silent. She didn't want to keep working for the *Evening Echo* for a few more years, and then settle down and give it all up. She wanted to be a newspaper woman, a good one, like Marta Raines, whose name appeared nearly every day above this or that news story in the great London paper, the *Daily Record*. She wanted all the excitement and glamour of a job on an important paper, one whose circulation soared into millions, instead of the precarious 15,000 of the *Evening Echo*. Marta Raines, she thought resentfully, must have begun somewhere, and why not on a local paper ? Getting a foothold was only a matter of luck, and when you want something as badly as Ann wanted journalistic success, surely luck must smile and beckon just once ?

Ann began to dress, putting on her new spring suit of green tweed, this being a special occasion. She was a tall girl, with curling dark hair and widely spaced eyes of brilliant hazel. A dusting of freckles over her short nose gave her a youthful, eager air; but her expression was mostly thoughtful and determined. She had just pulled the soft green felt hat down over one eye and was searching for bag and gloves, when Aunt Helen called up the stairs :

" Breakfast's ready, dear."

" Just coming, Aunt Helen."

She had better hurry, she thought. It was all very well to dream about the wonderful things that might happen if one resolved they should, but to-day was to be busy, filled with all kinds of small but— to her paper—important items.

She clattered downstairs, kissed Aunt Helen, and sat down with the sharp appetite of her age to bacon and eggs.

" Don't bolt it, darling," Aunt Helen said gently; " but when you've finished, look on the table behind you."

Dropping her knife and fork, Ann whirled round, her face shining with anticipation.

The little table against the wall was piled with parcels and letters, exciting parcels wrapped in tissue paper, letters fat and letters thin. And the top one of all was square and heavy and had a birthday card slipped under its ribbon tie.

" Happy birthday from Aunt Helen," it said.

Swiftly, with eager fingers, Ann unravelled the ribbon and tore away the paper. A fat book was revealed, its dark cover stamped with the words, *Journalism: Its Uses, Practice, and Opportunities. By Patrick J. Randall.*

For a moment Ann stared at it, then, like a child, she had leaped across the room and her arms were about Aunt Helen's neck.

" You darling ! " she said breathlessly. " You absolutely super-darling ! So you do think journalism is important, after all ? "

" On the contrary," Aunt Helen said calmly, " it occurred to me that this book would point out to you all the difficulties encountered by people with your ambitions, and discourage you in a way I don't seem able to."

Ann put back her head and laughed.

" Whatever your motive, you've given me something I've been saving up for this last three months. I can't wait to read it. Oh, Aunt Helen, I believe you're just an old fraud ! You're on my side, no matter how you try to hide it."

" What about your other presents ? There's something that looks very interesting from your Uncle James."

Ann glanced at her wrist-watch.

" I haven't got time now ; they'll have to wait until this evening. We'll have a lovely evening unpacking them together."

" Well, don't be later than you can help. I've got a chicken for dinner since birthdays don't come around every day."

Ann, draining her half-cold coffee, reflected that chicken had been the birthday dinner treat for the last ten years, ever since, in fact, Daddy and Mummy had been killed in a car accident, and seven-year-old Ann had come to live with Aunt Helen. And every year it tasted better. . . .

In those ten years, white hairs had appeared in Aunt Helen's hair ; the once lissom figure had filled out and become matronly ; there were lines and wrinkles on the face that Ann remembered as smooth and round. But Aunt Helen hadn't altered. From the day she had welcomed to her cottage at Harfold a small, bewildered child, stricken with grief over a half comprehended tragedy, Aunt Helen had been the same calm, kind, sweet person, mending and cooking, planning little treats, buying birthday and Christmas gifts for her dead sister's daughter. A week before birthdays, she wrote secretly to all the relatives, near or distant, ensuring that there should be a good pile of presents and cards for little Ann Thorne. At Christmas the process was repeated. Yes ; to motherless Ann, Aunt Helen had been an entire family. And now, on her seventeenth birthday, Aunt Helen had, even while denying it, bowed to an ambition that was like a consuming fire. She had capitulated to the printer's ink that Ann always swore ran in her veins instead of blood.

A sudden rush of love for her aunt swept over Ann, and she hugged her again.

" You *couldn't* have made me happier ! You're the most superb, the most miraculous aunt a niece ever had."

Aunt Helen smiled at her exuberance.

" Run along with you. You'll be late."

Riding her bicycle along the leafy lanes that led from Harfold to the country-seaport town of Meffingham, where the *Evening Echo* had its offices, Ann craned her neck for a glimpse of Britain's newest battle-cruiser, the *Berenice*, which had docked yesterday. Battleships, on rare occasions, put in at Meffingham, where there was an auxiliary naval repair shop, and these were times of great excitement to the townsfolk. Naval officers and sailors came ashore and spent money. Hotels, shops, garages, knew a brief moment of prosperity. It had been Ann's job yesterday to write nearly a column about the arrival of the *Berenice*.

It was still there, in one of the twin locks, a slim, grey, powerful looking craft. As the road took a loop towards the shore, she could see the sailors standing about her decks, the glint of gold braid as an officer raised an arm, a little feather of steam floating from a working winch. In her class, the *Berenice* was the pride of the service, and Ann had been thrilled by a conducted tour over her, the previous day, and the opportunity the fine ship offered for a descriptive article. Ann had, she told Aunt Helen loftily, " rather spread herself " in that article.

The offices of the *Evening Echo* lay up a narrow passage leading from the main street of Meffingham. A tumbledown old building housed them, a building that shook and shivered and threatened to fall apart whenever the old-fashioned rotary presses began to grind out their columns of news and features and advertisements.

Leaving her bicycle parked at the kerb, Ann went inside and made her way up to the first floor, entering with casual familiarity the dusty, dark, untidy apartment grandly labelled on the door " News Room." Two youths were feverishly banging on dilapidated typewriters. A middle-aged, discouraged-looking man sat at a desk apart, correcting proofs, while an aproned boy, sucking a toffee, waited to take them to the composing room. A shelf below the only window held a volume marked " Assignment Book," and to this Ann went, turning its tattered pages until she came to this day's date.

She saw that her name had been written against four items : the reopening, after repairs and decorations, of the local art gallery by the mayor ; a Women's Club luncheon, at which old Lady Carbridge was to speak on " Chicken Rearing for Pleasure and Profit " ; an exhibition of embroidery and pottery made by the county's Guild of Crafts-women ; and a Women's Institute tea to welcome back the vicar after an illness. She sighed as she transcribed the assignments into her notebook. The same weary old round! The same list of trivialities, from which one laboured to extract in writing some freshness or new angle. When, oh when, would the opportunity ever come to write something big, something that was important to newspaper readers all over the country? *Would* that opportunity ever come, or must she, as Aunt Helen insisted, remain in her narrow groove, trying to pump up an enthusiasm for events that long ago had lost the charm of novelty?

They had paid her, she reflected, fifteen shillings a week when she first came to this office, an excited, ambitious child of sixteen. Now she received the princely salary of twenty-five shillings, but her work had not changed by one iota. Mothers' meetings, school concerts, amateur dramatics, an occasional wedding or funeral—they had all to be reported in flattering or soothing terms.

The man at the desk—he was Tom Allan, chief reporter—looked up from his proofs and said, " Ann, just a minute."

" Yes, Mr. Allan ? "

" That guild exhibition. The editor's sister is showing something—pottery, I think—look out for it, and give it a special mention, will you ? "

" Yes, Mr. Allan."

" And get a few words from the vicar after the tea."

" Yes, Mr. Allan."

One of the youths looked up from his typewriter and made a friendly salute.

" Hiya, kid ! "

" Good-morning, Bill."

Bill Morgan was red-headed, freckled, energetic, and liked to think of himself as one of the reporters one sees in an American newspaper film. He wore his hat well to one side, affected laconic slang, worked hard at the business of appearing tough, and had a heart of gold and a wide humanity of outlook that were easily plumbed by the first-comer. In one respect he stood equal with Ann. He burned with ambition and resolution to make something of his life. He, too, dreamed of Fleet Street and the London papers. Every now and again he would bombard the editors of these with letters, tearing up the polite regrets that came back with a laugh and a toss of his red head.

" Six out of seven of them will be kicking themselves some day," he would say to Ann. " The seventh will be rubbing his hands and chortling because he took a chance and put me on his staff. I'll get there, Ann, never doubt it."

" So will I," Ann always answered, not a bit disturbed by his amused glance.

To-day, noting the look of bored discontent with which she swept the room, he asked, " Feeling the drag ? "

" It's my birthday," Ann told him. " I'm getting old without getting anywhere. Oh, I wish something would *happen* ! "

" Happy returns," Bill said perfunctorily. Then, as a bell clanged in the distance, grew louder, swept past and diminished, he grinned. " Well, you get your wish. Some one's haystack is afire. I'd better get on my trusty mo'bike and follow our gallant firefighters. Want that looked into, Mr. Allan ? " he asked, raising his voice.

" Suppose so," Tom Allan said, not lifting his head. And just then the telephone rang. Ann picked up the receiver, said " *Evening Echo*—news room," in what she hoped was the professional manner, and listened to a voice coming to her from somewhere. And, as she listened, her face changed, flushed, jerked towards the chief reporter.

" Mr. Allan . . . Mr. Allan ! "

" Yes, Ann ? " he asked, lifting disillusioned eyes.

" The fire is in the *Berenice* . . ."

" *In the Berenice* ? "

" Yes. It's Smith from the dockside paper shop calling. He says they're getting the fire-float out."

Tom Allan looked at Bill Morgan and shouted suddenly, " Well, what are you standing there for ? Get on out and make it fast. Let's have something —anything—for the first edition."

Ann watched with envious eyes as Bill Morgan dashed out of the room. It was just her luck to get the first news of a story, and then see some one else sent to cover it. With a sigh that seemed fetched straight from her brogues she prepared to go about her day's work.

Outside in the street the townspeople were

hurrying down to the little dock. Their feet made an uneven clatter on the pavement and the air was alive with voices, exclaiming, speculating, thrilled with the excitement of the moment. And from the sea a plume of black smoke was rising and spreading, beaten landwards by the brisk April breeze.

Ann said, " Oh, hang ! " and went off to the Art Gallery, where the mayor gazed at his suddenly depleted audience with an expression of cross frustration. It was difficult to be dignified and declare the gallery " well and truly reopened " to a small group of friends, each of whom was obviously torn between loyalty to the mayor and a desire to get down to the *Berenice* and see what there was to be seen. After the futile little ceremony the mayor detained Ann and made much of her, so that, in pity for him, she determined to use the phrase " before enthusiastic crowds " in her report.

She hurried back to the office to write it for the first edition, for there was still the Craftswomen's Guild to fit in before lunch, and discovered Bill Morgan sitting on his desk, smoking a cigarette and looking thoroughly disgruntled.

" Another flat tyre," he said, in answer to her questioning. " Oh, there was a fire all right. Started in the galley and spread to a ladder. But it was all over in five minutes. Such is life in Meffingham. Even the fires go out in discouragement."

" Never mind," Ann said comfortingly. " It's a better front page lead than the political situation."

" Yes," said Bill gloomily.

Twice more Ann came back to the office that day and banged out her stories on the typewriter. After the last assignment she was free for the evening, for the Women's Institute tea report would be held over until the next day, being too late to catch the last edition. She would be home in good time for the birthday chicken dinner after all.

At least, that is what she told herself cheerfully as she left the office, to have her cheerfulness dashed by discovering that the rear tyre of her bicycle had a puncture. And she had no time to wait for it to be mended.

" Have to take the bus," she thought, thinking ruefully of the three-mile ride there, the wait for a bus to return to Meffingham, the further ride back to Harfold, and Aunt Helen's disappointment at her lateness.

"Oh, well," thought Ann, with a shrug. "She knows it's all part of the job."

She left her machine at the cycle shop and caught the small, old-fashioned bus that trundled out to the hamlet where the tea was being held. It was fairly crowded. A few workmen, knocking off early, jostled housewives from the country districts whose baskets were full of parcels. Ann was glad to get one of the narrow seats to herself. and she sank into it and gave herself up to dreams and longings. But at the next stop a sailor got in and sat beside her, taking off his hat and planting it on his knees. Ann could see written in gold lettering on the ribbon, H.M.S. *Berenice*.

With a friendly smile she turned to him and asked, " Is the fire quite out, and did it do much damage ? "

" It's out," said the sailor. " As for damage— well, we might have been gutted if it hadn't been for my mate. He found out where it started and acted prompt-like."

" Where *did* it start ? "

" In the galley. Sabotage, that's what that was," said the sailor, his round, ingenuous face solemn and indignant.

" Oh, come," protested Ann, smiling at him. " Sabotage ? Surely not ? You're joking, aren't you ? "

" Joking ? Not on your life, Miss. That fire was delib'rate, as we can all tell you. Why, it was my mate 'oo found all the oily rags and shavings stuffed into the fuel cupboard. There isn't never anything but oil-drums in them cupboards, and they was inspected only last night. You can take it from me, Miss, there's a bit o' dirty work going on, and now we've got the whole ship guarded like she was a new-born baby, as you might say."

Ann's heart was beating high and fast and her cheeks were flushed. The sailor was young, little more than a boy, but his voice was full of conviction, and his eyes were honest and direct.

Trying to steady her voice, Ann said, " Does every one in the ship know it was sabotage ? I mean, isn't it being kept a secret ? "

" Oh, well," said the young sailor, shrugging his

shoulders, "you can't keep nothing dark in a ship, you know. It'll all come out in the Court of Inquiry, anyway. There'll have to be a court, you see. Always is, when anything like that happens. Of course, I wouldn't go about shouting the odds, but to a young lady like you it don't make any difference, I reckon. I got to get out at the next stop."

"You've friends in these parts?" Ann asked. She wanted to get hold of his name, but if she asked him outright she knew she would put him on his guard. He helped her with innocent comradeliness.

"My ole mother. She lives in Little Stinford. You might know her, p'r'aps, Miss? Mrs. Harding?"

As Ann shook her head. He added, "Don't often get around this way, so I got special shore leave for the night. Leave stopped for all the other chaps, but I was lucky. Like to see the old lady when I get a chance. Well, good-night, Miss, if you're going farther."

"Good-night," said Ann, and watched him edge his way out to the platform and swing lithely into the road.

For the rest of the journey she sat with her brain on fire. Out of the skies, it seemed, without warning, a news story had dropped into her lap. A *big* news story. The special recognition, the particular sensitivity of the born journalist, told her that this was a story for which any news editor would give his back teeth. And what was she to do with it?

Loyalty and training told her to ring up Tom

The sailor was young, little more than a boy, but his voice
was full of conviction.

Allan, so that he could arrange a special late edition and news bills. But ambition said, "What's the use? He'll ring up the big London papers and spill it to them all, and they'll pay him a few shillings linage. I won't get any credit. No one will know that I found the story. This is my chance—but can I take it?"

The bus was reaching her stopping-place, and still her mind was in a whirl. Indecision tore at her, while fidelity to the firm that employed her fought with the knowledge that at last she had something to offer the great powers of her dreamed-of world, something that would bring her to their notice, that might result in a step along the path she so longed to follow.

She sat through the tea at the Institute, talked automatically with the mothers, secured a brief interview with the convalescent vicar, and went out to wait for the Meffingham bus.

It was dusk, and the little village street was alive with sound—the women bidding each other good-bye, arranging other meetings, gossiping in the Institute door. Children played about the cottage gardens, shouting and laughing, and a flock of ducks made a sudden sortie across the road and flopped into a pond with much loud quacking.

But Ann heard nothing. She was listening with her inner ear to temptation. And temptation said, "What do you really owe the *Echo*? You've worked hard and faithfully for it, and it will keep you slaving away for years, giving you an annual five shillings rise, and taking you nowhere. Use some common sense. Don't you realize this may be the chance you're always praying for ? "

And in her heart she answered, " But the *Echo* people have taught me my job. I wasn't much use in the beginning, but they were patient with me, and kind, and showed me the ropes. I owe the *Echo* this story as the least of repayments."

Temptation said, " Nonsense ! Or if that's your attitude, you must be content to stay in Meffingham for ever. Only by a scoop like this can you expect to get out, and such a scoop may never come your way again. Are you going to throw it away out of sentimentality ? "

" No," Ann said, unaware that she was speaking aloud. " No, I'm not."

She looked around and saw the post office a little farther up the street. The red paint of a telephone booth gleamed gaily against its rustic exterior.

She had two separate shillings, two sixpences, and a handful of coppers—enough for a call to London. Going into the box, she asked for Trunks and demanded a long-distance call.

" Central 90000. The *Daily Record*, please," she said huskily.

When the *Record* answered, she asked to speak to the news editor, giving her name and address firmly and clearly. Some one asked her what she wanted, but she insisted that she must speak to the news editor first. " I've got a story I must talk to him about," she said.

And presently a pleasant, impersonal voice said, " Alan Weaver speaking. Who is that ? "

" This is Ann Thorne, of the Meffingham *Evening Echo*. I've got a story, but this isn't linage. This is exclusive, and I want to sell it."

" What's the story ? "

" It's sabotage in one of our newest battleships. I've got all the facts. What will you pay me for a story like that ? "

There was a pause, and then the famous news editor of the *Daily Record* said, " *What* did you say your name was ? "

" Thorne," Ann said patiently. " Ann Thorne. I'm a reporter on the Meffingham *Evening Echo*, but I've just picked up a fine story and I've got it to sell. Do you think you want it, or shall I offer it to the *Daily Banner* ? "

" No ; don't do that. Look here, if the story stands up and we can check on all facts, we'll give you ten guineas for it. That's only *if* everything is okay, you understand ? "

Her effort at self-control and cool bargaining had left Ann faint and shaky. " I understand," she said, while her legs trembled and her throat grew dry. She had done it ! She had pulled it off ! She had sold a scoop to a national newspaper, and now they would know her name and remember her as a girl with a nose for news !

Weaver said, " Hold the line a minute, and I'll get some one to take you down."

She heard him shout, " Blaydon. *Blaydon !*

Take this call on number six." To the operator he said, " Put this call on number six, please. Miss Thorne," he added, " we won't keep you a minute. I'm having you transferred. Please give all your facts to Mr. Blaydon."

In another minute a voice said, " Hallo ! May I have your name and address, please ? Thank you. Now what is your story ? "

" It's sabotage in the new battle-cruiser *Berenice*," Ann told him, and heard him catch his breath. " Here are the facts."

Slowly, sometimes prompted by a question, she told him about the fire which it seemed was already old news. She told him of meeting the sailor, Harding, in the bus and what he had said. She told him the village where Harding's mother lived, the fact that all leave was stopped in the ship, that a guard had been posted, and that a Court of Inquiry was expected. At the end of her recital, Blaydon said, " Will you hang on a minute longer ? I must speak to the news editor."

Ann said, " I'm afraid my three minutes must be up, and I haven't any more change."

" That's all right. Transfer the charges to us and we'll take them. I'll tell the chief operator."

Ann was thrilled from her head to her feet, thrilled with the excitement of finding and selling a story, thrilled with the courtesy and efficiency of the staff of the *Daily Record*, thrilled that she found herself taken seriously.

Blaydon's voice said, " Sorry to keep you waiting.

I'm leaving at once for Meffingham, shall get there about eight. Can I see you ? I may need your help. You see, I don't know that district at all, and one can work much faster with some one who knows short cuts and so on."

" How are you coming ? "

" Car. Portsmouth Road and fork left at Fareham, isn't it ? "

" That's right. You'd better pick me up at home," directed Ann, and told him how to get to Aunt Helen's cottage.

" I'll be there by eight-thirty. And listen," added Blaydon, a trifle diffidently ; "keep your mouth buttoned, won't you ? We want to keep this exclusive."

Ann said indignantly, " I'm a reporter."

" Of course. So you are. And you sound like a good one to me. Well, I'll be seeing you."

Dazed with happiness, Ann came out of the telephone booth. So she sounded like " a good reporter " ? Well, that was what she was, what she was going to be—a great and famous reporter.

If only the thought of the *Evening Echo* would stop nagging at the back of her mind the world would have been perfect.

CHAPTER TWO

YOUNG MAN FROM FLEET STREET

"AREN'T you going to change into a frock for dinner?" asked Aunt Helen, as Ann, tidied and washed but still in her green suit, came into the dining-room.

Ann hesitated. She hadn't yet said anything to Aunt Helen about the afternoon's activities, for although she had been on the verge of blurting it out several times, she found herself unable to formulate the necessary phrases. It seemed too difficult to remark airily that she had withheld an important story from her own paper and sold it to the *Daily Record*, and that a young man from the *Record* was coming to see her in consequence. Aunt Helen was the soul of honour, and she might not understand.

Ann said, "Well no, Auntie dear. As a matter of fact, I've got to go out again presently on business."

"*On your birthday night?*" Aunt Helen's tone was incredulous. "But didn't you explain that you always stay at home on your birthday, and that we have a little celebration? The Browns and Hallidays are coming in later to give you their birthday wishes.

Couldn't Allan have given the job, whatever it is, to some one else ? "

" This isn't a job for the *Echo*," said Ann, with colour mounting in her face. " It's for the *Daily Record*, and a reporter called Mr. Blaydon is going to call for me at half-past eight."

Aunt Helen wrinkled her delicate nose and looked at her niece in doubt.

" What on earth do you mean, Ann ? What are you talking about ? Why should a reporter from the *Record* . . .?"

Half shamefaced, half proud, Ann began to explain. So anxious was she to justify herself that the words tripped over her tongue, and she finished her little speech in a rush and flurry.

There was a brief silence. Then Aunt Helen said firmly, " You've done wrong, Ann. And it's not too late to telephone Allan and let him know all about it."

" Oh no, I can't do that ! I gave my word to the *Record* that I wouldn't say anything. Oh, darling, don't you see—don't you *see* that this is my chance ? At last I've got my chance."

" Fiddlesticks ! " said Aunt Helen brusquely. " Chance, indeed. Why, the *Record* will just pick your brains and then, when the excitement has all died down, forget all about you. And the *Echo* will remember what you've done."

" They won't forget me," Ann said furiously. " They won't because I won't let them. I've put my name over, and I'm going to follow it up with other stories. Aunt Helen, I sold this story for ten guineas, more than a month's salary from the *Echo*. I'll sell them others, you'll see."

With a face that refused to soften and smile, Aunt Helen led the way to the dinner table and began carving the birthday chicken. Miserably, yet with that inner excitement buoying her up, Ann followed. She tried to eat her dinner, tried to manage the trifle that followed the chicken, tried to drink her coffee, but every nerve was strained for the sound of a car outside the cottage, for her first glimpse at a real reporter from a real newspaper. What would he be like? Would he be a more assured edition of Bill Morgan—hat on one side, careless clothes, and a tough manner of talking? Oh! would he never come? The clock hands went round with a deliberation that was maddening.

At last there came the squeal of brakes, the slam of a car door, footsteps on the path, and a knock on the door. Ann flew to open it. . . .

Her first reaction was one of intense disappointment. Blaydon, of the *Daily Record*, was a quiet-looking, almost nondescript person. He wore an impeccably tailored suit of dark grey, with a soft hat set on his head in a manner both unobtrusive and conventional. In the light from the hall his face appeared quite unremarkable, and he was young—not more, thought Ann, than twenty-one or twenty-two. It was only when he spoke, with a confident self-assured address, that she realized he was not some dull business man.

"Miss Thorne?" asked Blaydon of the *Record*.

" Good ! Are you ready to come along with me ? There isn't much time, you know. We'd like this for the third edition, if possible."

" Y-yes," stammered Ann. " Of course. W-won't you come in for a minute while I get my hat ? "

" Thanks," he said, and stepped inside, taking in the cottage interior with one comprehensive glance.

Ann said, " This is my aunt, Miss Canfield. Aunt Helen, this is Mr. Blaydon, of the *Daily Record*. Perhaps he would like a glass of sherry while he's waiting for me."

At the foot of the stairs she turned.

" I won't be a minute."

But when she stood in her bedroom Ann was afraid the minute would stretch itself out indefinitely. She was shaking with nervous excitement. This seemed the biggest thing that had ever happened to her, and she tried to brace herself to meet it. She must appear calm and collected, as if she were used to dealing with big news stories, as if to-day were merely part of her normal routine.

It was only when she had pulled herself together sufficiently to run downstairs again that she realized her guest was also excited. He was toying with a glass of sherry, making some sort of conversation with Aunt Helen, but his face lit up when Ann appeared, and he snatched his hat from the chair where he had thrown it.

" Ready ? That's fine. Well, good-night, Miss

Canfield. I'll try not to keep your niece out too late, but this is one of those front-pagers, you know. Miss Thorne can be a tremendous help to me."

Aunt Helen said drily, " She'll like that."

It was then that Ann, in a rush of remorse, swept across the room and enveloped her aunt in a hug.

" Don't be disappointed about the party, darling. This is something that may make all the difference to my life. We can have a party to-morrow night, if you like."

" Good luck to your story," Aunt Helen said unexpectedly. She smiled for the first time that evening. " I'll try to keep the party going until you get back. If not, we'll have it some other night."

" You sweet thing ! "

And then Ann was sitting beside Blaydon in his car, confusedly acknowledging an introduction to a man who sat behind, and who carried what she recognized as a Press camera.

" Now then," said Blaydon, " where are these docks of yours ? We must look 'em over first."

Ann directed him to the small dockyard, and when they arrived at its dark quietude was able to show them the *Berenice*, a long, cubist chunk of blackness, lighted here and there by an uncovered scuttle and by her red and green riding lamps.

Blaydon parked the car, motioned the camera-man to join him, and began to prowl about. Once Ann saw him approach the watchman standing on guard beside a lowered gangway, but the watchman evidently had orders to watch his tongue as well as his ship, for Blaydon presently left him, a discouraged droop to his shoulders. He came back to the car and said, " Nothing much there. Where's the village where this sailor you told us about lives ? "

" Little Stinford," said Ann. " It's about four miles from here."

" Okay." Blaydon climbed into the car again, and the camera-man, whose name appeared to be Mick, resumed his rear seat.

Mrs. Harding's cottage in Little Stinford was easy to find, and Blaydon leaped from the car, ran up the front path and knocked on the door. The sailor himself opened it, and the two men began to talk, gravely and quietly. Ann could see the sailor shaking his head, while Blaydon seemed to be urging and demanding at the same time. Presently the sailor pulled the door shut behind him and walked down the path and out into the road with Blaydon. Together they paced up and down, too far away for Ann to hear what was being said. When at last they shook hands, something seemed to pass from Blaydon's hand to the sailor's, and the reporter came back and got into the car.

" Very tricky," he said, as he let in his gears and began to turn the car. " Scared stiff of saying anything, and frantic that his name mustn't be used. If it were, the poor chap would probably be kicked out of the Navy. But he's told me what I want to know, and now, if the chaps in the office have got a statement from the Admiralty, we've got a first-class story."

" I'm glad," Ann said, smiling.

He glanced down at her.

" Well, it's thanks to you, you know. It was pretty bright of you to spot a piece of hot news like that and let us have it so promptly."

" I *am* pretty bright," Ann told him. " Though there's not much chance of using one's brightness in a one-horse town like Meffingham. I want to get to London."

Blaydon drove in silence for a while.

Then, " You wouldn't really like it, kid," he said. " You just don't know how hard the work is, how monotonous, how gruelling. It's all glamour to you at the moment—the sort of glamour they put over in films of newspaper life. Scoops. The front page. Headlines. Your name over a story. That's what it looks like to you, isn't it ? "

Ann said impatiently, " Of course not. I'm not soft in the head. I know it's hard work, without much glamour, and I know it's difficult to get on. But I don't care about all that. I want to work on a London paper more than anything in the world. Ever since I was old enough to think of my future, I've wanted that. You must know how I feel ; you must have felt like that yourself when you were first trying to get a foothold in Fleet Street."

" Well, I did, of course. But it's different for a girl, I should think."

" It's *not* different," cried Ann passionately. " If you know in your heart and mind, in your very bones, that you were born to be a journalist, it doesn't matter in the slightest if you're a man or a girl. There's always work—there *must* be—for some one who's as keen and willing as I am. The thing is to get a first look-in, and that's difficult, I admit."

Blaydon shot a quick look at her in the half darkness of the car.

" Not so difficult if you've a friend at court," he said.

" But I haven't," Ann pointed out disconsolately. " I don't know a single soul in Fleet Street except you." She caught her breath. " Mr. Blaydon . . . I suppose you couldn't . . . you wouldn't . . . ? "

" Wouldn't what ? "

" Speak to your news editor about me ? Tell him that I'm good and that I want a job ? I know how hopeless it is for an unknown person to try to get work up there, but if there were some one to help . . . some one who believed . . . mightn't it make all the difference ? "

" Mm-m." Blaydon sounded abstracted. " Look here, we shall have to find a phone. I must get my end of the story over."

" You can use ours," Ann said eagerly. " We're nearly home now."

The party was over, and Aunt Helen had gone to bed when Ann let the two men into the cottage and showed Blaydon the telephone in the sitting-room. He snatched up the receiver.

39

" I want a transferred call to Central 90000. Roger Blaydon calling the *Daily Record*. Okay, I'll hold on."

He grinned at Ann over his shoulder.

" This call won't appear on your phone bill. The office accepts it and pays for it."

" I see," said Ann, tucking this useful piece of knowledge away in her mind.

Presently Blaydon was speaking again.

" Phillips ? Blaydon here. Yes, the story stands up and I've got all the possible facts. Couldn't get on board, but talked to the chap whose mate found the evidence. No names no pack drill, of course. Some one ready to take it down ? "

For the next ten minutes he was busy pouring out in crisp language a circumstantial story of the fire in the *Berenice*. Ann, listening with all her ears, noted that nothing was imagined or unduly exaggerated, whilst the important facts of the story were given their full value and the details expertly worked in. She was amazed at the close observation the reporter showed—the small touches describing the sailor, his mother's cottage, the layout of the village, the guard set on the ship. He seemed to have missed nothing.

She thought, " That's training. But I can do it ; I could do all he's done, with a little more experience and practice. Oh, I do so wonder if . . . no, I mustn't think of it. I'll go and make some tea for them. They'll probably like something before going back."

Blaydon and Mick, who seemed to be the most silent man Ann had ever met, were pleased with her tea and a piled plate of Aunt Helen's special scones. And presently Ann reverted to the subject uppermost in her mind.

She said, a little timidly, " Mr. Blaydon, do you think you could do what I asked you ? Speak to your news editor about me, I mean ? Ask him to give me an interview soon if I take a day off and go to London."

Blaydon looked across the room at Mick with a cocked eyebrow, and Mick gave a stolid nod.

" She'll do," he said gruffly, speaking for the first time since entering the cottage.

" I think you'll live to regret it," Blaydon said hesitantly. " Even if it comes to anything, that is, and naturally I can't make any promises. But I will have a word with Phillips, and I'll write you what he says."

" You *will* ? " Ann was breathless with excitement. " Oh, thank you, Mr. Blaydon. Thank you most frightfully. And I'll see that *you* don't live to regret it, anyway."

He rose and made a sign to Mick.

" We must be on our way. If anything else comes to light about the *Berenice* you'll let us know at once, won't you ? And you can expect to hear from me before the end of the week."

And then Ann was left alone in the cosy, lamp-lit room, free at last to examine her birthday presents and read her cards and notes. But she unpacked

41

and looked at the gifts abstractedly, her mind busy with the exciting events of the evening. It seemed too good to be true that Roger Blaydon was actually going to ask the news editor of the *Record* to give her a chance. Blaydon must be pretty important, she thought, to be rushed out on what he himself admitted to be a big story. Probably his word would carry a lot of weight.

" Ann Thorne, of the *Daily Record*," she whispered to herself, and her heart gave a little leap of pure joy. " That's how I'll be introducing myself soon. Ann Thorne, of the *Daily Record*."

Her heart was to leap again the next morning when, cycling to work on Aunt Helen's machine through the Meffingham streets, she caught sight of the *Daily Record's* news contents bill.

SABOTAGE IN BRITAIN'S NEWEST
CRUISER

said one.

And another shouted :

ATTEMPT TO FIRE BATTLE-CRUISER.
EXCLUSIVE.

Ann knew such a sense of shock that she nearly fell off her bicycle. Never before had any work of hers been important enough to merit a news bill ; in fact, such a situation had never occurred to her. Now her reaction was more frightened than happy.

Suppose the story were denied ? Suppose the sailor, telling her, in his innocent excitement, the true tale of the fire, should be found out and get into terrible trouble ? Only she and Blaydon knew his name, and wild horses would never drag it from her ; but would Blaydon remain silent if there were some tremendous row about it ?

She bought a paper and stood at a street corner, scanning its sensational front page.

FOURTH SABOTAGE ATTEMPT IN SIX MONTHS.

FULL STATEMENT FROM ADMIRALTY.

OILY RAGS AND SHAVINGS IN GALLEY LOCKER.

HEROIC WORK BY RATING.

GUARD ON SHIP: COURT OF INQUIRY SITS TO-MORROW.

There they were, the screaming headlines, sub-headings, a photograph of the *Berenice*, and a long story, " By Roger Blaydon," with a date-line, " Meffingham. Monday."

Well, thought Ann, she had certainly started something. Whatever the outcome, she had at least distinguished herself on her seventeenth birthday by selling a front-page story to the *Daily Record*.

She dropped the paper into a litter-bin before going into the office. It might look a little suspicious

43

to be seen walking into the *Echo* news room with a copy of the *Record* under her arm. Some one might connect her with that front page.

The news room was in an uproar. Bill Morgan, his hat so far back on his head that it seemed held on only by will-power, was shouting down one of the three telephones. Another reporter rushed through the room with his hands full of Press Association " flashes." Tom Allan scribbled with a sort of concentrated venom, and the quick glance he bestowed on Ann held something strange and inimical in its depths.

He said, " Don't bother with that Women's Institute stuff. Shan't have room for it. And the editor wants to see you."

Ann caught her breath. To be sent for by the editor, old Mr. Storeman, was an event so unusual that no one could receive the summons with unshaken calm. Mr. Storeman worked in an office on the ground floor, was rarely seen by his employees, and was held in respect and awe by every one in the building. It was known that he was a Fellow of the Institute of Journalists, and it was rumoured that he had once written and had published a book about newspaper production. It was with difficulty that Ann turned and made what she hoped was a casual exit from the news room, for her knees seemed turned to jelly, and she was aware that the eyes of every one in the room were on her.

Her discomfort was increased when she found that Mr. Storeman was not alone. Seated beside him was the proprietor of the paper, bluff hard-eyed Samuel Harrington.

" Come in, Miss Thorne," old Mr. Storeman said, his faded blue eyes stern on her face. He did not ask her to sit down, and Mr. Harrington neither smiled nor spoke. Both men seemed concentrated on a copy of the *Daily Record*, which lay on the editor's desk between them.

And at last the editor spoke.

" Miss Thorne, have you seen this story on the front page of the *Record* this morning ? "

" Y-yes," said Ann faintly. " I read it a little while ago."

" Of course. Miss Thorne, I must ask you this. Do you know anything about the story ? Do you know how the *Record* got hold of it ? "

So it had come ! She was discovered in disloyalty to her own paper, and there was nothing to do but admit it. Well, why not admit it ? The Meffingham *Echo* seemed so small and silly and unimportant after her contact, last night, with a real newspaper, with real newspaper men.

Her chin lifted and she said quietly and steadily, " Yes, Mr. Storeman. I sold the story to the *Record*."

Mr. Harrington said, coldly and crisply, " At what time did you find the story, Miss Thorne ? "

" In the early evening, Mr. Harrington. About five, I think."

" In time, in fact, for us to have got out a special edition and news bills ? "

" Yes," admitted Ann. " I suppose so."

" And you deliberately turned your back on your own paper—we could have put circulation up by at least five hundred with the first news—and sold it to a London paper. Have you anything to say ? "

Ann had so much to say that she had trouble in keeping her thoughts and ideas and feelings from tumbling out, all mixed up and incoherent. She wanted to explain, but the hard-eyed proprietor and the worried, reproachful old editor seemed hardly the sympathetic audience needed by headlong, thoughtless youth.

After a minute she said, " It was because I want to get to London. I want to work for a big news-paper and . . . and . . . this seemed to be my . . . my chance."

She knew that was bald and crude. She sensed the outraged stiffening in the attitude of the two men she confronted. But it was the best she could do, for tears were pressing now in her throat, behind her eyes. She wanted to cry, " I don't care ! I don't care ! I *must* do the best I can for my dream. . . . I must make it come true somehow."

But the trouble was that she *did* care. The inter-view with her two chiefs had brought suddenly to her the enormity of her behaviour. She had held in contempt a paper which had always treated her well, that had trusted her, that had given her the status of an esteemed and valuable journalist. And she had betrayed it.

Twisting her fingers, stammering, she said, " I'm
. . . I'm sorry, Mr. Storeman."

It was Samuel Harrington who answered her.

" It's a little late to be sorry, Miss Thorne.
The damage is done. This organization has no
place for disloyal employees, so I am afraid we must
consider your association with us at an end. The
cashier will give you a month's salary in lieu of
notice. Good-morning, Miss Thorne."

" Good-morning, Miss Thorne," echoed the
editor, and Ann said almost inaudibly, " Good-
morning," and rushed from the room.

Upstairs, in a silence that could be felt, she
began to clear out the drawer of her desk, tearing
up old papers and notes, setting aside a little pile
of cuttings of her best work. And at last Bill Morgan
lounged over and sat on a corner of her desk.

" So it *was* you ? " he asked.

Ann nodded miserably.

" Thought so. One of the printers saw you
talking to a *Berenice* sailor in the bus and gave us
the tip. Good work, kid," said Bill Morgan unexpectedly. " Very nice work, and I hope you get
something from it. Been fired ? "

Ann raised eyes full of tears to his.

" Yes, Bill."

" So what ? This isn't the only news rag in the
world. In fact, if it died to-morrow I don't suppose
any one would miss it. What are you going to do
now ? "

" I'm going," Ann said, clearly and suddenly,

47

" to have a crack at Fleet Street. I have to wait for a letter. But it'll come any day now, and then I'm off to work for a real newspaper. You'll see."

" I won't be long behind you," Bill Morgan assured her. " I only need a chunk of luck, just like you found last night, and I'll be on my way to join you."

But the letter that was to come " any day now " seemed unaccountably delayed. After breaking the news of her dismissal to Aunt Helen, after the tears and arguments that followed, Ann settled down to wait for two or three days for word from Roger Blaydon. She cycled about the country, looking all the time for some other story that might be suitable to offer to the *Record*. When Aunt Helen was out, she would lift the telephone receiver, keeping a careful finger on the release bar, and dictate long, imaginary news stories, crisp and authoritative, along a dead line—practising for when she would actually be talking to a telephonist-reporter at the other end. She studied the pages of the *Record* with close attention and scribbled away at invented happenings, modelling her style exactly on the brief, brightly informative style of those fortunate reporters who already had a job with the paper. And still she waited.

It was hard, that waiting. It was hard not to dash into the road and snatch the letters from the postman's hand whenever he approached the cottage. It was hard to prevent herself from demanding that he should search his packet of mail for other people to make sure he hadn't missed the all-important note from Roger Blaydon. It was hard to get trivial, chatty news from old school friends, to receive envelopes that were never stamped on the back with the magic words *Daily Record*.

Ten days went by, ten days of such concentrated hope, fear, despair, and wretchedness that Ann felt her nerves would soon break down altogether. Aunt Helen kept quietly in the background, but Ann was aware of her disapproval of the whole situation, and her belief that Roger Blaydon had just been making empty promises.

Then one morning Ann met Bill Morgan in the streets of Meffingham.

" Hallo ! " he exclaimed. " Come down to look at your home town ? Or haven't you started to set Fleet Street on fire ? "

With sudden resolution, her pride flaming, Ann said, " I'm going up to-morrow to have an interview with the news editor of the *Record*."

" Well, I wish you luck, kid."

" Thank you, Bill."

At supper that night Ann said quietly, " I'm going to London to-morrow, Aunt Helen."

" To London, dear ? "

" Yes. I want to see some one there. In fact, I'm going to look for a job."

" Darling, aren't you being rather obstinate and silly ? It's obvious now that your reporter friend never thought you had a chance of getting work on the *Record*. He was just playing with you. Wouldn't it be better, if you're so set on this journalist idea, to try for work on one of the Ralliford papers across the bay ? If you got a post with one of those, we might be able to afford a tiny car for you to get to the office in."

"No," Ann said firmly. "What's the good of going to Ralliford ? It would only mean the same sort of job I had on the *Echo*—no future, no chance at anything better. I'm going to see Mr. Phillips, and, if he won't take me on, I'll go and see all the other editors."

"If they'll see you," Aunt Helen pointed out.

"Well, if they won't, they'll at least hear my name."

Aunt Helen sighed.

"Well, Ann, it's your own life."

"Yes," agreed Ann fiercely. "It *is* my own life, and I know what I want to do with it. Darling, don't look so sceptical and depressing. It's not that I want to leave you, but there's something inside me that drives me, and I've got to pay attention to it. It's terribly important to me."

There were tears in Aunt Helen's eyes, but she smiled as she said softly, "I try to understand. You can borrow my silver fox, if you like."

That was the disconcerting thing about Aunt Helen. She fought you, strongly and determinedly, until you said something that seemed to hold a secret key to her heart, And then she gave way, usually with a gesture of such generosity and sweetness that you found yourself disarmed and penitent.

50

At that moment, Ann almost felt she would give up the trip to London, give up the whole ambitious dream of newspaper fame. If the issue had been just a little less vital to her, she would have capitulated at once and accepted Aunt Helen's advice, whatever it was. But this was the one thing on which she had to stand firm.

" It's lovely of you," she said, referring to the silver fox. " It'll bring me luck—I know it will. Thank you a thousand times."

So that Ann's green suit was given an air of opulent smartness by Aunt Helen's new and beautiful silver fox, the next morning, when its wearer boarded the train for London.

All the way up Ann rehearsed to herself just what she would say to the news editor of the *Daily Record*, letting her imagination run free as she decided what he would answer. Every now and again she was seized by a little spasm of anger against Roger Blaydon.

" Empty promises ? Playing with me ? I'll show him ! He'll be surprised when he finds what I can do without his help. It was a hateful thing to do, knowing how keen I was, and I shall never, never forgive him. And that's a sort of pity, because I liked him and we might have been friends."

When the slums of London, that smoky, grimy, south-of-the-river introduction to the City, began to slide past the carriage windows, she found her heart beating violently and her hands clammy with nervousness. Wasn't she, perhaps, being stupidly bold, rushing up from the heart of the country to demand a job on one of the greatest newspapers the world had ever seen ? What would she say or do if she couldn't get an interview with any one in authority ? How would she earn her living—how, indeed, would she ever hold up her head there again— if she had to return to Meffingham confessing failure ?

Shyness and uncertainty flowed over her when she stood outside the great modern edifice of the *Daily Record* in Fleet Street. Through the swing doors she caught a glimpse of long, shining counters, chromium chairs, uniformed receptionists, silver-buttoned page-boys dashing here and there. A never-ending stream of people pushed in and out of the great doors, some young and alert and prosperous-looking ; some old and shabby ; some nondescript. Cars drew up outside and discharged portly, abstracted business men ; taxis disgorged impatient, hurried young men ; a small, vivid girl in a red leather coat pulled a sports car to a stop, jumped out and said to the doorman, " I'll take it away in a minute, George. Must put this stuff over." She disappeared into a lift and was shot upwards.

And at last Ann remembered that she, too, was entitled to respect. Hadn't she sold the story of the sabotage in the *Berenice* ? She entered and said to a receptionist, " I'd like to see Mr. Phillips, please."

The man pushed a pad of paper towards her.

" Just write your name and business, please, Miss, and then take a seat over there."

Ann wrote her name, then paused. How could

she put her business down ? How phrase it ? To confess her actual intention would bring, she was sensible enough to realize, an instant refusal. At last she wrote " of the Meffingham *Evening Echo*," and went to sit on one of the leather and chromium chairs beyond the counter. She saw a page-boy take her slip of paper and go off with it, and composed herself to wait.

There was so much to see and note that the waiting period seemed short, although actually it was nearly twenty minutes before a young man bowed before her, saying politely, " Miss Thorne ? I'm Fred Storm, of the editorial staff. I'm sorry the news editor is engaged. Is there anything I can do for you ? "

But Ann knew what this meant. She had been sent to talk to importunate callers herself when they called at the *Evening Echo* to see the news editor or chief reporter. Courteously, yet with quiet firmness, she said, " I'm sorry, but my business is with Mr. Phillips personally. When can I find him free to see me ? "

" If you'll just give me some idea of your business, I could go and find out," the young man called Fred Storm said, recognizing at once the impossibility of fobbing off this pretty, self-possessed girl with specious excuses.

Ann thought fast, knowing how much depended on her answer.

" Please tell Mr. Phillips that it concerns the sabotage in the *Berenice*," she said finally.

Fred Storm looked impressed.

" You have some further news ? "

" I'd rather discuss it with Mr. Phillips," Ann said, and gave him her sudden, radiant smile. " If you'd just remind him that I am the Miss Thorne who sold you the story—the first story of the sabotage —I'm sure he'll find time to see me."

Mr. Phillips, it seemed, was not so heavily engaged that he could not find time for the Miss Thorne who had given his paper an exclusive story that was still remembered.

She followed Fred Storm into a lift and was whisked to the second floor ; went after him along a corridor, across a huge room, cluttered with desks, at which sat a score of young men and two women, typing frantically, or talking into telephone mouthpieces, or scribbling hastily on large pads of paper. Small boys dashed about, their hands full of papers. A pipe-smoking man in shirt sleeves, his eyes hidden beneath a green shade, popped his head out of a door and yelled, " Greenbaum ! Where the devil is Greenbaum ? Boy, find Mr. Greenbaum and send him to me."

And at last, at the far end of that enormous room, they halted outside a door. In gold letters on a frosted glass background, the words " News Editor " seemed to glare at Ann. Terror took her by the throat and knees, and her heart seemed to drop right down into her small suede shoes. But pride lifted her chin, and her face, if pale, was composed.

Fred Storm knocked, put his head round the door and said something. Then he turned and said, " Go right in, Miss Thorne. Mr. Phillips will see you at once."

Carefully controlling her breathing, trying desperately to look unimpressed and casual, Ann walked into the office of the news editor of the *Daily Record*.

CHAPTER THREE

" . . . OF THE RECORD "

GREGORY PHILLIPS was a square, dark, rather harassed-looking man. He sat at a large desk that was piled with every kind of paper and book and yet managed to look neat and efficient. The glance he turned on Ann as she entered was intelligent, uncompromising, and full of swift appraisal.

He saw a slim, large-eyed girl, charmingly dressed in green and a silver fox fur, a girl whose face was both eager and abashed.

"Sit down, Miss Thorne. I won't keep you a minute. I must just get this stuff finished and out."

For a minute he scribbled busily, while Ann was at liberty to examine the room, the big poster that shouted "ACCURACY FIRST!" The maps of Europe, stuck about with tiny flags; the shelves crowded with books of reference; the two telephones on the desk. Another poster, pasted on the wall by the door asked "WHO? WHEN? WHAT? WHERE? WHY?" which, she supposed, must mean the essentials of a news story. And at last Gregory Phillips finished writing, pressed a buzzer, and handed his work to the small boy who answered.

" Chief sub," he said briefly, then turned to Ann. " Now, Miss Thorne, I understand you have some further news of the sabotage story."

" Oh no," Ann said quickly. " I didn't say that, I assure you I didn't. I only mentioned the *Berenice* to remind you who I am."

" I see. Then what is it you wish to see me about ? "

His tone was so terse and businesslike that Ann, for a moment, was tongue-tied. Colour rushed up to her cheeks as she wondered if Phillips thought she had got into his presence by false pretences.

She said, " Mr. Phillips, I—I'm a very good reporter. If you'd like to see cuttings of my work, I've got some here. I—I came to ask you if you would give me a chance to work for the *Daily Record*."

Gregory Phillips shook his head with decision.

" I'm sorry. I haven't a vacancy at all, and there are several highly experienced journalists waiting until there is one."

" But *I'm* experienced," Ann cried desperately. " And I'm keen. Oh, I would work so hard for you, if you'd only give me the opportunity ! And you'll have to admit I do know news when I come up against it."

" I admit it freely," Phillips assured her. " But a reporter needs more than the ability to recognize news to hold down a job on a paper like this. He needs tact and decision and a comprehensive know-ledge of all sorts of things, from foreign politics to

57

the latest fashions. He needs a long experience of newspaper work. And you—forgive me, Miss Thorne—are very young."

" Even the young have to begin somewhere," she told him.

" Yes, yes. But a few more years on your present paper will supply you with a more saleable working equipment. I advise you to try to enlarge your knowledge of your own paper's workings—learn how to do make-up of pages, study type faces, discover how print is composed and picture blocks made. Get a good working idea of the technical end of newspapers, if you can. And, of course, we shall always be glad to consider any work you like to send us."

Ann listened to that speech with her heart sinking into her shoes. Naturally, she might have known, jobs on great national papers aren't handed out to girls of seventeen, with only one year of newspaper work to recommend them, no matter how keen and ambitious they may be.

She got to her feet, fighting to keep the tears from her eyes and throat, as she said, " Well, thank you for seeing me, Mr. Phillips. I mustn't waste your time."

She found her hand swallowed up in a hard, close grip, and turned to the door.

" The only thing is," she added wistfully, " the fact that I can't take your advice."

" You can't ? Why not ? "

" Well, you see, I was dismissed from my paper

for selling you the *Berenice* story. Good-bye, and thank you."

" Hey ! " cried Phillips, as her hand was on the door-knob. " Come back. What did you say ? You got fired for selling us the story ? "

Ann nodded miserably.

" They said I cost them a lot of circulation, and that I had been disloyal. . . ."

Gregory Phillips stroked his chin, his eyes suddenly thoughtful.

" That puts a different aspect on it. We don't like people to suffer through doing us a service. Look here, wait a few minutes, will you ? I want to have a word with my assistant, Weaver."

He went out of the room and Ann stood rooted to the carpet. Had she found, all unsuspecting, the key to unlock the door of dreams ? Would Phillips change his mind and give her a job ? Would he— oh, would he ? She thought, " I'll faint, or do something just as silly, if he keeps me in suspense much longer."

And then Gregory Phillips was back in the room, motioning her to sit down again.

" Do you know what it means to work ' on space,' Miss Thorne ? " he asked.

" Of course," said Ann eagerly. " It means you get paid for what work you have in the paper."

" Exactly. Well, now, we can't offer you a staff job. We haven't got one to offer, and if we had it would have to go to some one else. But if you like to accept a retaining fee of a guinea weekly, and come in on the space basis, you can begin next week. I warn you that you'll probably half starve to begin with."

Ann's eyes were shining, and she felt a laugh welling up inside her, a laugh of incredulous relief.

She said, " Oh, thank you, thank you, Mr. Phillips ! I can't tell you how happy you've made me. And I shan't starve for long. If I did, I wouldn't be worth anything to you, would I ? "

Phillips smiled at her enthusiasm.

" I'll get some one to show you round the office and try to find you a desk somewhere."

He pressed his buzzer and said to the copy boy who came in, " Send me in any reporter who isn't busy."

While they waited, Phillips said, " Report to Mr. Weaver, the assistant news editor, when you start. Next Monday ? Right. And keep your eyes and ears open for anything you think might make news. We like our staff to bring in ideas, as well as work on those of others. Ah, Blaydon. Busy ? Good. Just show Miss Thorne over the office, will you ? Fix her up with a desk and—oh, of course, you two have met before, haven't you ? Didn't you cover the *Berenice* story ? "

" Yes," said Roger Blaydon, offering a welcoming hand. " So you're really coming to work for us, Miss Thorne ? That's grand. Come along then, and I'll show you what makes us tick."

" Thank you," said Ann coldly, her expression distant. She turned to Gregory Phillips.

"You've been very kind. I won't let you down, Mr. Phillips."

"I'm sure you won't," he said, and then she found herself outside in the news room again, Roger Blaydon's hand under her elbow.

"But this is marvellous! I mean, you coming up here and getting a job with us all off your own bat. I say, I hope you didn't think I'd forgotten my promise to you? You see. . . ."

"Please don't trouble to explain," Ann said icily. "I'm really not in the least interested."

"But won't you let me . . .?"

"I said, I'm not interested," she interrupted.

Roger Blaydon shrugged, looking at her with eyes that were both hurt and annoyed.

"Oh, very well. Just as you say, of course. Now, this is the main news room. That long table over there, where all the men are working, is the sub-editors' table. The man at the head of it is James Wilkie, the chief sub. You'll have to meet him, but that will do when you join us. This little desk here I know is unoccupied, so it ought to do for you. I'll have a boy fit it up with paper and pencils and so on. You do your telephoning from any of that row of booths just over there. Now you'd better see the library. You'll find it a most important room as far as work's concerned."

Ann could hardly repress a gasp of surprise when she saw the huge room, with its tall racks of envelopes each bulging with cuttings about every subject under the sun. The distant half of the library was given up to pictures and photographic blocks, all tucked tidily away and filed in alphabetical order. The chief librarian, Mr. Bronson, smiled at her and shook hands.

" If there's anything you want to find out, Miss Thorne, just come and ask me, or any of my assistants."

Ann thanked him, her eyes roving over the shelved walls, where books, encyclopædias, directories, foreign travel guides, and rows of biographies of important men and women rose high above her head and stretched as far as she could see.

She thought, " I can't take it in, it's all so stupendous. But I mustn't let them see I'm impressed ; I mustn't act like a country cousin."

So that when Blaydon asked her if she'd like to see the presses and the composing room, she said languidly, " Yes, it might be interesting."

In Meffingham, Ann had been accustomed to seeing three linotypers and a handful of printers at work. She wasn't prepared for the row upon row of linotype machines, with their scores of operators, and the almost uncountable printers and minders. The great presses, still now since edition time had not yet arrived, lay like shining and powerful beasts, couched in their beds of concrete.

" These are the newest and most efficient electric multiple rotary presses in the world," Blaydon told her. " They cost nearly half a million pounds to lay down and are the wonder of the publishing world. So don't look at them with that bored expression.

He looked at her with laughing eyes, and Ann instinctively stiffened.

" I didn't know I was looking bored. Of course, I think they are magnificent."

" Good. Now you'll have to have some visiting cards engraved. If you'll write your full name on this slip of paper, Mr. Pierce, the head printer, will have some done for you. They'll be ready when you start work. When are you coming ? "

" Next Monday," Ann said.

" Right. I'll keep an eye open for you. And at the moment, you'd better come and meet Alan Weaver—you'll be reporting to him."

Alan Weaver said, " So you're the young woman who gave us a world beat on the *Berenice* story ? Welcome to the office." He was a thin, sharp-faced, stooping man, and he wore a green shade over alert grey eyes. But his smile for Ann was kindly, and she felt herself liking him at once.

At this moment the girl in the red leather coat came up and said, " Oh, Alan, I clipped this from a local rag when I was on that Gravesend job. Do you think there might be something good in it ? "

Weaver read the cutting she handed him, and said, " Seem to have seen something about it before. Try the library, but if there's nothing there, it might be worth looking into. Oh, by the way, this is Miss Ann Thorne, who is coming to work for us. Miss Thorne, Miss Marta Raines."

So this was the famous Marta Raines! Ann's

glance was a little awed. She saw a small, blonde woman, in her middle twenties, not pretty, but attractive because of her open, intelligent expression, and wide hazel eyes that held a spark of fun in their depths.

" How do you do ? " Ann asked, a little timidly. Marta Raines put out a friendly hand.

" I'm glad to see you. I hope you're coming prepared to stick up for your rights against this slave-driver ? " She indicated Weaver. " He'll work you all day and all night and even on your days off, if you'll let him. You have to be firm."

Ann was nearly overcome with surprise that a reporter could be so impudent about an august person like an assistant news editor. She had yet to learn the atmosphere of equality and informality that pervades the relationships of the staff of a great newspaper.

" It's a bit tricky, starting on a new job," Marta went on. " So, if there's anything you need help with, come and ask me."

" Thank you very much."

And now she was walking back down the long room, where telephones pealed without ceasing, where men and women dashed about, looking absorbed and hurried, where heads were bent over desks, typewriters clattered, voices shouted " Boy ! " or " Copy up ! " and a brief laugh from two chatting colleagues only seemed to add to the air of intense occupation and tension.

Roger Blaydon said, " I've got half an hour to spare. Won't you let me take you for some tea ? You might like to see the café we all go to."

But Ann was still smarting over Blaydon's broken promise, and she said, " No, thank you. I must catch my train home."

" All right. Then we'll be seeing you on Monday. Good-bye, Miss Thorne, and congratulations."

Ann couldn't help a note of malice in her voice as she answered, " I told you I should get here, didn't I ? It was silly of me to ask for your help when I didn't really need it."

" I wish you'd let me explain. . . ."

" It's quite all right. Good-bye, Mr. Blaydon."

She was carried swiftly to the ground floor in one of the luxurious lifts, and went out into Fleet Street with her head in the clouds and her feet treading on air.

" I'm Ann Thorne, of the *Record*," she told herself, lifting her face to the thin drizzle of rain and smiling with a radiance that startled passers-by. " Ann Thorne, of the *Record*. It's wonderful. It's marvellous ! I can't believe it's true. And what will Aunt Helen say now, I wonder ? "

Aunt Helen took it very quietly.

She said, " Well, I suppose it makes you happy, dear. What are your plans ? You'll have to live in London, of course ; have you thought where and how ? "

" Oh, I expect I shall be able to find some sort

of hostel, or something like that," Ann said airily.
" I think a hostel, anyway, until I find out how much
I can earn. It won't be the same every week, so I
shall have to live very quietly until I can strike an
average."

Aunt Helen said, " I can let you have a small
allowance, darling."

" Oh, *no*, Aunt Helen," cried Ann instantly.
" It's most terribly sweet of you, but I don't want
that. I want to earn my own living entirely by myself, at the job I like best to do. Don't worry, dear.
I expect I shall be making heaps of money quite
soon."

" Well, I wouldn't count on earning a fortune ;
and you'll have to save a little, you know, for clothes
and holidays and emergencies."

" I'll send you some every week for you to save
for me. That will be a good plan, won't it ? "

" Excellent," said Aunt Helen.

Her face was sad and her voice suddenly low and
indistinct, and Ann knew a pang at the thought of
leaving this dear person who had been so much to
her all these years. She dropped on the rug beside
her aunt and put her head down on the comfortable
lap.

" You don't think I'm an ungrateful beast, going
away from you like this, do you ? I don't mean to
be, and I shall miss you every minute. It's simply
that I can't help myself—I *have* to go."

A tender hand smoothed her hair.

" I understand just how you feel, Ann. Would

you like me to sell the cottage and come up to London and live with you ? "

But Ann knew that Aunt Helen would never be happy away from her beloved cottage, away from her villagers and simple friends, away from her garden, which responded so faithfully and colourfully to its owner's " green fingers." Aunt Helen was country born and bred ; she would be miserable in noisy, sophisticated London. To offer to go there was, Ann realized, a gesture of supreme sacrifice. She caught at her aunt's hand and kissed the finger-tips, one by one.

" You're a heavenly person, you know. There's no one in the world like you. But I won't drag you up to a city life you'd hate, in fact, I won't hear of it. You'd be so unhappy that it would make me unhappy. No ; you stay here, where I can picture you being always the same, and I'll come down for holidays and what week-ends I'm allowed off."

There was relief as well as sadness in Aunt Helen's sigh.

" Well," she said practically, " we'd better start looking over your clothes, and see what wants mending and pressing and cleaning."

The rest of the week seemed to fly. There was so much to do and so little time in which to do it. On the Saturday, when she was shopping for last minute necessities in Meffingham, Bill Morgan hailed her.

" Hallo, kid ! What's all the news ? "

" I thought you would have heard. The whole

county seems to know about it," laughed Ann. " I've joined the *Daily Record*, and I start work on Monday."

" That's terrific ! Well, when you're sitting on top of the world, covered in glory, don't forget the hometown boy-friend, and say a good word for him. Though maybe I'll be sitting right alongside you, because I'm going to get to Grub Street too, and soon. Anyway, good luck, Ann, and good stories. I'll be watching for your work."

" Oh," said Ann deprecatingly, " I don't suppose they'll let me sign my stories right away. I shall have to wait a few months for that. But if I do anything startling, I'll send you a clipping, and you can show it to every one on the *Echo*, saying ' local girl makes good.' "

" I'll do that."

And then, all suddenly it seemed, it was Sunday evening, and Ann and Aunt Helen were driving along leafy lanes in the station taxi. Ann had selected the most promising looking in a column of advertisements and arranged by post to stay at a hostel for business girls in Baker Street. She was to pay a guinea a week for a cubicle and two meals a day.

" So that everything else I earn will be mine," she explained to Aunt Helen. " In fact, I shall probably have a nice big bank balance this time next year."

" I hope so, darling."

There were tears from both of them as they

parted at Meffingham Station. Ann couldn't help hers, for never before had Aunt Helen seemed quite so dear, and never before had she looked so forlorn and in need of comforting.

"I'll write lots," she promised huskily. "Good-bye, darling Aunt Helen, and thank you for always being so good to me."

"I love you," Aunt Helen said quietly, as if the little phrase explained everything, and Ann's tears flowed faster.

But, as the train slid away from the old brown town, and the fields, in the dusk, took on a misty, faëry quality, the first, fierce jubilation returned, and the wheels of the train revolved to the rhythm of a short sentence, a sentence that repeated itself over and over again, all the way to London. . . .

"Ann Thorne, of the *Daily Record*. . . . Ann Thorne, of the *Record*. . . . Ann Thorne, reporter on the *Record*. . . ."

CHAPTER FOUR

THE FRONT PAGE

IT was a little shyly that Ann pushed through the great swing doors of the *Daily Record* the following morning. The desk porter looked at her inquiringly, and she said, " I'm Ann Thorne. I'm starting work here to-day."

" Oh, yes, that's right, Miss. You're to go straight up to Mr. Weaver."

A little round-faced lift boy, known to every one in the building as Pugs, saluted smartly and shot her up to the editorial floor, where she crossed the big news room and went to stand by Alan Weaver's desk. He looked up from slitting open letters from an enormous pile, and for a moment his eyes were puzzled. Then they cleared, and he gave her a brief smile.

" Of course. Miss Thorne. Well, I've nothing for you at the moment, but I understand Blaydon found you a desk. You'll see your hours of duty and days off posted with the others on the notice board. You haven't got a story in your pocket, have you ? Things are a bit quiet."

Ann shook her head regretfully and went off to study the notice board. Her duty hours, she saw, were from eleven to nine all the week, with all day

Saturday off. There were other notices—an outing organized by the *Record* Sports Club ; a tattered piece of proof paper printed with typographical and literary rules for reporters ; an instruction about obtaining railway passes ; a commentary on the previous day's paper by the editor, distributing praise and blame with strict impartiality. Ann wondered what the editor was like, if he were an awe-inspiring person, ready, like Jove, to hurl lightning and thunderbolts on offenders. She didn't, she realized, even know his name, and it seemed silly to ask some one the name of the editor of her own paper.

For an hour she sat at her desk, idly reading an evening paper of the night before. There was, she gathered, no assignment book, such as she had been used to on the Meffingham *Echo*. Evidently jobs were handed out by Alan Weaver, for she had seen him call one or two reporters over to him, seen them grab their hats and leave the news room immediately. And presently a boy came over to her and said, " Will you see Mr. Weaver, please, Miss ? "

The assistant news editor handed her a clipping of a court report from a late edition of a last night's evening paper.

" Go and interview the wife in this case and get her side of the story," he said. " It should make a good little human interest special."

" Yes, Mr. Weaver."

Ann took the cutting away with her and lingered at her desk a minute to study it. A man and his wife had lived for the last few years in the same house

without speaking a word to each other. When they
had wanted to communicate they had left notes on
the table. The wife had applied for a separation,
but the magistrate had told her to go home and
try to make it up with her husband. The address
of the house was Gleaning Road, Brixton.

Brixton ? She wondered where that might be,
but could not bring herself to ask anybody. It
might be just around the corner, and she would get
laughed at. Oh, well, better get going. This was
her first assignment on a new and important paper,
and she must—she *must*—do well at it.

Going out of the building into Fleet Street, she
walked slowly westwards, scanning the bus boards
to see if any of them were going to Brixton. But
none of them even mentioned it. . . . And at last she
put her pride in her pocket and approached the point
duty policeman at the end of Fetter Lane.

" Brixton, Miss ? Well, if I was you, I'd walk
down through the Temple to the Embankment and
take a tram. Most of them go to Brixton from
there."

Gleaning Road, Brixton, turned out to be a
narrow squalid street of small and dirty houses.
Grubby lace curtains, half screening the aspidistra
of respectability, hung in most of the windows, and
the couple of feet of front garden to each house
produced nothing but sooty and discouraged laurel
bushes, or a grimy shrub or two. Ann pushed open
the gate of No. 7 and knocked on the door.

It was opened by a large, square woman, whose

bad-tempered face was framed by a row of curling-pins. She stood, arms akimbo, regarding Ann inquiringly.

"Mrs. Batts?" asked Ann. "I'm Ann Thorne, of the *Daily Record*." (At last she had really said it!) "I wonder if you would like to tell us something about your life of silence with your husband? Give us your side of the story, you know?"

The face of Mrs. Batts assumed a vicious malevolence.

"Ho!" she said loudly. "So you're a reporter, are yer? One of them as put me name in the paper last night, I dessay. I'd jest like to know what business it is of your'n wot me and me old man does or doesn't."

"Well, you see," Ann said, "you're in the news. The story you told the magistrate yesterday interests every one. That's why I'm here."

"Yus, I see. Snoopin' lot o' busybodies, that's wot you newspaper people are. Well, I ain't got nothin' to say and nor 'as my ole man. And if you ain't orf my doorstep while I watch yer, I'll set me dorg on yer, so I will."

Ann stood astounded and speechless. Never in her life had she met with such a rebuff. In Meffingham and its environments she had only to mention the name of her paper to be invited inside and treated with gratifying respect. She had never envisaged some one who had no awe of the power of the Press.

Mrs. Batts said, "Go on, 'op it. And if yer mention me name again in the paper, I'll sue yer, see?"

It was a depressed and apprehensive Ann who travelled back on the tram to the Embankment. She walked into the office with a desolate heart, wondering how she was to confess to Alan Weaver that she had failed to get a story on her first assignment.

But Alan Weaver was unexpectedly casual.

" Never mind, Miss Thorne. Some people just can't be interviewed. Did she say anything at all printable ? "

Humour flashed to Ann's rescue.

" Everything she said was quite unprintable."

" I see. Well, here's a card to attend a show of paintings by a Spanish refugee. I believe he had difficulty in smuggling his work out of the country. Run down and see the pictures and get a talk from the artist, will you ? Just a couple of sticks will do."

Ann secured what she considered a first-class interview with the Spanish artist, Pablo Plañes, and she wrote it and her opinion of his work with great care. There were, it seemed, no more jobs for her, and, after hanging about the office for a few more hours, she was allowed to go home to the hostel in Baker Street. Her mood hovered now between despair at muffing her first assignment and delight at pulling off her second. It was a long time before she fell asleep in the narrow truckle bed that took up so much room in her tiny cubicle.

First thing in the morning she dashed out to a newsagent and bought a *Daily Record*, arranging to have it delivered to her daily at the hostel. And her breakfast grew cold as she opened the paper and anxiously scanned its pages. When she came to the seventh page her eye was caught by a heading, and it seemed that her heart must stop beating with fright and humiliation.

FIVE YEARS OF SILENCE

Man and Wife write 112 Notes to Each Other.
Yet they live in the same house.
By MARTA RAINES.

And there was a long interview with Mrs. Batts, together with comments from Mr. Batts, with headlines that splashed themselves across three columns, and even a photograph of the dissenting pair. Marta Raines had taken over Ann Thorne's work and made her usual success of it !

In a panic, she whipped through the paper, looking for her story of the Spanish painter. She found it at last, a pitiful little paragraph, tucked away in a corner, with hardly a word from her own writing left in the text.

" I'm a failure," she thought desperately. " That's what it is. To think that Marta Raines could get an interview with that terrible woman, while I just ran away when she shouted at me. I just haven't got the knack, I suppose. Mr. Weaver, all of them, they'll all be laughing at me, and I don't think I can bear to face them. And Roger Blaydon will be laughing the most. How can I bring myself to go back to that office ? "

The girl who sat beside her at the breakfast table, a pretty red-haired girl with laughing eyes, looked up and spoke to Ann.

" The housekeeper told me that you're a reporter on the *Daily Record*." The laughing eyes grew awed. " I think that's marvellous ! I should love to be a reporter, but fate insisted that I should make a better stenographer. I'm Molly Andrews, by the way, and I work in a solicitor's office in the City."

At the admiration so frankly expressed in the voice and face of Molly Andrews, all Ann's courage came flooding back, and pride stiffened her resolution, suddenly made, not to let one failure spoil her life's ambition. She smiled and said, " I'm Ann Thorne. Yes, it's fun being a reporter, but I expect you're an awfully good stenographer. We both have our uses."

" That's true. Is that the *Record* ? Is there anything of yours in it to-day ? I'd love to read it."

But Ann, hating to confess to her miserable little paragraph, hastily folded the paper and said, " No, there's nothing of mine in this edition."

" Well, I must be going," said Molly, rolling her napkin and collecting bag and gloves. " Do you like the movies ? There's a grand film with Clark Gable and Carole Lombard at the ' Gigantic ' this week. We might go together one night when you're not too busy."

When Ann set off for Fleet Street, an hour later, she went with the warm feeling in her heart that she had made a friend.

No one at the office said anything about her failure of yesterday. Alan Weaver gave her a brief smile and said, " I'll have something for you presently, Miss Thorne," and Ann went to her desk and read through the morning papers. Once Roger Blaydon passed and said, " Getting on all right ? You'll soon settle down."

Ann was repenting of her cold treatment of him, and now she gave him a smile and said, " I hope so. I seem to have blotted my copybook already, but perhaps it isn't so serious."

" Oh ? What did you do ? "

She told him of the story she had muffed, and how Marta Raines had secured and written it.

" Don't worry about that. It might have happened to any of us," Roger Blaydon comforted her. " Marta's a walking miracle when it comes to dealing with people of that class. She has us all beat."

And presently Marta Raines herself came over.

" Please don't feel badly about that story," she said, her voice friendly. " I really got it by a sort of trick. You see, I happen to know Mrs. Batts's brother-in-law, and I made him come with me and help talk her over. You'll be getting some contacts like that yourself soon, and things will come easier to you."

Ann was given three jobs that day : small ones, worth only a few lines, but each time she brought her little story off without difficulty, and she went back to her hostel feeling happier.

Writing to Aunt Helen, she stressed her delight

in her work, describing the office and her colleagues with painstaking detail.

"And I've made friends with a girl who lives here. Her name is Molly Andrews, and we are planning to go to movies together, so, you see, darling Aunt Helen, I shan't be lonely, though, of course, I miss you all the time."

For the next few days things were rather slack for Ann. She was given only the most trivial jobs to do, so that most of her time was free to study the methods by which a great newspaper is run. Once she spent an enthralled hour in the long glassed-in room where the telephone reporters worked, listening to them taking down stories from all over the world —America, Australia, China—and from the network of correspondents spread all over Britain. Weaver allowed her to examine the news " flashes " from the Press Association, Reuters, the Exchange Telegraph, that seemed to come into the office every few minutes. She learned, with Roger Blaydon's help, to translate " cable-ese," that strange language used by editors to instruct reporters abroad, and by reporters sending in stories from the far corners of the earth. She hung about the sub-editor's table, watching " copy " being slashed and rewritten, pencilled over with mysterious instructions to the printers, and sent away by hurrying boys. She went up to the studios and saw camera-men come dashing in, to develop and print their pictures within a few minutes and send them down, still wet, to the art editor. And all this knowledge she filed in her mind as added working equipment that was, one day, to make her an " ace " reporter.

" Come and have some tea," Roger Blaydon invited her, one afternoon. Ann was glad to go, for she needed something to take her mind off the depressing fact that her first week's pay cheque added up to the minute sum of two pounds, three, and six.

" I don't see how I'm going to save anything from pay like this," she thought discontentedly. " When, oh, when, is Mr. Weaver going to send me on a big story ? If I once get a chance to distinguish myself I might get better jobs to do and earn more. It's not that I care so frightfully about the money, but I do want to be taken seriously as a journalist."

Roger Blaydon took her to a little café a few doors up Fleet Street from the *Daily Record* office.

" All the *Record* people come here," he explained. " Each paper seems to adopt a certain café and make it its own, and editors wanting this or that staff member know just where to send a boy to look for them."

Ann said, " You'll think I'm an awful fool, Mr. Blaydon, but I don't know what our editor's name is."

He laughed.

" Couldn't you call me Roger ? We don't go in much for misters and misses in this street. Well, his name is Grimthorpe—John Grimthorpe—and you'll probably never meet him except at the annual office dinner, or if you do something wonderful or extra bad. He's a nice chap, though ; every one likes him."

They ordered tea and scones, and Roger pointed out to Ann various members of the *Record* staff, some of them celebrities, like Lord Ambleton, who contributed a daily half-page of London gossip. He was a little dried-up man with a wizened face ; at the moment he was wolfing poached eggs on toast and drinking numerous cups of tea. In a far corner was a thin-faced, spectacled man, deep in a book ; he was William Harris, the editor's personal secretary. Gregory Phillips himself had slipped out for a brief moment of relaxation from news editing.

" Ann," said Roger, when she had poured their tea and was ready to give him her attention. " Won't you let me explain now why I didn't write to you as I promised ? "

" Of course I will," said Ann, who was fundamentally incapable of holding a grudge for long. " I'm sorry I was so horrid to you, anyway, and I'm sure you had a good reason."

" I certainly had. You see, the day after I got back from Meffingham, the assistant to our Paris man fell ill, and I was sent over there for ten days to help out. I'd only just got back when Phillips sent for me, and I found you sitting in his office with him. I hadn't forgotten my promise, so you could have knocked me down with a feather when I saw you."

" I do understand," Ann assured him. " It was beastly of me not to have listened to you before, but

I had built so much on hearing from you and then, when no letter came, I just had to assume you'd forgotten all about me. And that made me frightfully angry."

" Well, so long as I'm forgiven now, everything's all right again. What have you got to do this evening ? "

" Cocktail party for Alma Grayson, the Hollywood star, at the Savoy. It'll be rather fun seeing her in real life."

" I hope you won't be disappointed. And don't forget that these parties are publicity stunts, so try to get a different angle from that of every one else."

" Yes ; I mean to," Ann said earnestly. " I thought of asking her about her views on women—try to get her to say something catty and startling, you know."

" Good girl, that's the idea. You've got all the makings of a top-class reporter, you know, and you'll get there some day."

Ann glowed at the praise from a fellow reporter who was " top-class."

At six she went off to her cocktail party filled with confidence in her ability to get something " different " from Alma Grayson for *Daily Record* readers.

The party was being held in a first floor suite, and the two long rooms, when Ann arrived, were already thickly peopled with journalists, publicity agents, film actors and actresses, and a producer or two. Ann hovered about Alma Grayson for half an hour, waiting for an opportunity to get her alone for a minute, and, when that minute came, she plunged straight into her questions.

Alma Grayson, who was beautiful, vivacious, and incurably stupid, fell straight into the trap laid for her and delivered herself of some trenchant witticisms at the expense of her own sex. Ann, who knew better than to produce notebook and pencil in front of a victim, tucked the star's remarks away in her mind, thanked her, and withdrew into a corner, and was just finishing transcribing the interview into her book when a pleasant voice said, " You look awfully busy—can I get you an ice, or a drink, or something ? "

Ann was excited and thirsty, and she smiled up at the young man who bent over her and said, " I'd love a lemonade, if there is such a thing. The still kind, not a fizzy one."

" I'll see what I can do," said the young man, and shouldered his way through the crowd towards the buffet. He came back after a minute with a tall glass.

" Ginger-ale is the nearest they have. Will that do ? "

" Splendidly." Ann took the glass from him and sipped at it. " That was awfully kind of you. I'm so thirsty—it's all this steam heat, I suppose. I'm not used to it."

" You don't look as if you are," he said, sitting down beside her. " You look as if you had been transplanted from the country, with that skin of yours and your clear eyes. Are you a journalist ? "

" I'm Ann Thorne, of the *Daily Record*," she told him, thrilling as she still did whenever she introduced herself. " I was just putting down my interview with Miss Grayson. I've got a good one."

He smiled at her enthusiasm.

" I'm glad to meet you, Miss Thorne. I'm Geoffrey Falcon-Arbutt, if the name conveys anything to you."

Ann sat up straight.

" It does, if you're any relation to Sir Frederick Falcon-Arbutt. I went to see him last week, to find out the truth about his projected amalgamation of Arbutt Steel and Consolidated Industrial Products. He's nice, but he wouldn't tell me anything," she added sadly.

" He's my father," said the young man. " Honestly, it beats me how you newspaper people get hold of these things. The whole deal was supposed to be deadly secret until it was concluded. They won't announce it to the Press until to-morrow, anyway, now that Dad's pulled it off. . . ."

He stopped dead, realizing by her widened, excited eyes that he had committed an indiscretion.

" I say—look here, Miss Thorne—I shouldn't have said that. Dad will have me shot at dawn. Could you just forget I even mentioned the wretched thing ? "

Ann shook her head.

" I couldn't do that. You've given me an important piece of news, you know, and I shall have to hand it on to my news editor."

"But . . . oh, heavens! Listen, you couldn't really . . . on a social occasion like this . . . pick a chap up and use his words against him ? "

"This isn't a social occasion for me. It's part of my work. I'm afraid I shall have to use what you just told me, though I'm sorry if it will get you into trouble. I don't see why you should worry, though. You said it will be announced to-morrow, which only means we have first news that the amalgamation has gone through. Some paper usually gets a scoop on a story like this, and this time it's the *Record*."

Geoffrey Falcon-Arbutt looked thoughtful. He lit a cigarette and stared at Ann through the smoke, while she looked back at him, her brilliant eyes expressing determination not to be talked out of using her suddenly acquired knowledge.

At last he said, "Would it do you any good personally to run the story ? "

"*Would it ?* I can't tell you how much good it would do me. It's just what I need, actually."

"Well, having let it out like that, and knowing you mean to use it whatever I say, I suppose I might as well tell you the whole thing. When the old man sees it in the *Record* to-morrow he won't be so wild if all the facts are straight."

"Oh, *would* you ? Would you really ? " Ann's face was flushed with thrilled gratitude. "That's wonderful of you ! "

"I don't seem to have much choice, do I ? " asked Geoffrey Falcon-Arbutt, with a wry smile.

"I say—look here, Miss Thorne—I shouldn't have said that."

" Well, would you like to take it all down here, or shall we go somewhere quieter ? "

" I suppose," Ann suggested diffidently, " you wouldn't come to the office with me ? We could be private there, and you could even wait and see the story, when it's written. You could make any corrections you thought necessary, couldn't you ? "

" All right. It seems a good idea. Let's go then—my car's out in the courtyard."

The pride and delight in Ann's heart threatened to choke her before she got out words that made Alan Weaver sit up and stare.

" Mr. Weaver . . . I've got Sir Frederick Falcon-Arbutt's son here in the office. That amalgamation has gone through, and he's going to give me all the details. . . ."

" *What ?* "

" Yes, really, Mr. Weaver. Look, he's over there by my desk."

" Well, I'm . . . look here, take him into that small room with the glass door. And get everything. *Everything*, don't forget. This is front page."

" And I've got some good stuff from Alma Grayson. . . ."

" Never mind about Alma Grayson. Get the amalgamation stuff. It's a story that affects thousands of speculators. I'll have to have a first edition re-plate."

Geoffrey Falcon-Arbutt kept his word, and gave Ann every possible detail about the stupendous business deal that had been engaging the attention of the public for weeks. He himself worked in his father's offices, so he had the whole thing at his finger-tips.

" I shall get hanged, drawn, and quartered for this," he told Ann, smiling ruefully. " But I think I've done the best thing, having let the cat out of the bag in the first place."

There was excitement and rush in the office while the front page was re-made to carry the amalgamation story as the lead. As Ann finished each page of her story, it was practically ripped from her typewriter, hurriedly "subbed," and rushed down to the printers. Gregory Phillips came in and thanked young Falcon-Arbutt, who, fascinated by the activity and strangeness of a newspaper office, asked if he might stay until proofs came up so that he could look them over for corrections. A disengaged reporter was told off to show him round, while Ann got busy on her film star story.

That, too, was received with acclamation by Weaver.

" Nice work, Ann." That he unconsciously used her first name gave Ann a tremendous thrill. " It'll make women sit up all over the country."

So there was Ann, trying to look calm and unimpressed, but bubbling over with the delight of successful achievement. When, at half-past seven, Weaver told her she might go, her cup of joy seemed overflowing.

She rushed back to the hostel, ate a quick meal, and invaded the cubicle of Molly Andrews.

" Let's go to the movies, shall we ? I want to celebrate."

" Rather ! I'd love to. What are we celebrating ? "

The whole story had to be told to Molly, who was almost as happy about it as Ann herself.

" It's wonderful . . . wonderful," she kept repeating, her blue eyes dancing with excitement. " I can hardly wait to see the paper."

" If we stay up till midnight we can buy a first edition," Ann suggested.

"Oh! let's do that. I adore buying to-morrow's paper to-night. It's like having a secret peep into the future."

So after the cinema the two girls went to an all-night café, stifling their yawns over coffee, and waited until the magic hour when boys would go round the room, crying, " Papair ! Papair ! *Daily Record ! Record !* "

And at last they came, and Ann snatched a paper from a newsboy and spread it excitedly over the table. Right across seven columns her financial story shouted its news. There were photographs of Sir Frederick Falcon-Arbutt and of Major Rees Alleyn, the president of Consolidated Industrial Products, and above the story ran the magic words, " Exclusive to the *Daily Record*. By a Staff Reporter.

" My first front page," Ann said softly. " Oh, Molly, I've never been so happy in my life. I've dreamed of this—and now it's happened."

" Something else has happened," said Molly,

who was studying the paper. " Look at this. You've made the front page twice in one go."

Sure enough, at the right-hand foot of the page was a photograph of Alma Grayson and a headline that ran, " WOMEN HATE EACH OTHER," says Hollywood star Alma Grayson. " There is no real friendship between women."

And now Ann's face was pale and her eyes like saucers. She simply couldn't believe such a thing could happen—that she could see her work twice on the front page of a newspaper on which she had worked for only a week.

Suddenly she fumbled in her bag for a pencil, found one, and scored heavy black lines round the two stories. Then, on a page from her notebook, she wrote, " I did both these stories. Love. Ann." Tearing the front page from the paper, she folded the note up in it and jumped to her feet.

" Let's find a post office. Isn't the one at Charing Cross open all night ? I want to send this to Aunt Helen. Then she'll *know* I was right to snatch at my chance when it came. Oh, Molly, I shan't sleep a wink to-night. Wake me up in the morning, will you ? "

But sleep Ann did, deeply and dreamlessly, to wake early and leap out of bed, full of happy energy, feeling that she would like to hug the whole world.

And in the office she had the delight of being congratulated by one after another of her colleagues, all of whom regarded her with a new respect.

Presently a boy came to her desk.

" Will you see Mr. Grimthorpe, please, Miss ? "

" Y-yes . . ." stammered Ann. " Of c-course. Where shall I find him ? "

" This way, please, Miss."

She was going to see the editor ! He had sent for her ! For a second a thought made her heart beat painfully. Suppose something were wrong with the story ? Suppose it had been denied by Sir Falcon-Arbutt ? What could she say or do ? But common sense came to her rescue as she remembered that all the other big daily papers had carried the story, " lifted," in their later editions, from the *Record's* exclusive one.

Now she was being ushered into a big, luxurious room, and her feet were sinking into a deep-piled carpet, while sunshine, pouring in through a wide window, dazzled her eyes. There were flowers on the great desk at the end of the room, and behind it sat a man, waiting for her to approach him.

" Mr. Grimthorpe ? " she faltered.

" Yes, come in, Miss Thorne. I thought I'd like to meet the newest member of my staff, especially one who gave us such a distinguished story. Congratulations ! "

John Grimthorpe was a middle-aged man, handsome in a grave and heavy manner. His hair had greyed into two wings on his temples, and his dark eyes were shrewd and kindly.

" Why," he said, as Ann stammered her thanks, " I had no idea our Miss Thorne was so young."

" I'm seventeen," Ann said, lifting a proud chin.

He looked impressed, but there was a twinkle in his eye.

" Tell me something about yourself."

Ann told him her brief newspaper history and of how she had been dismissed from the *Evening Echo* for selling the *Berenice* sabotage story to the *Record*.

" It was a blessing in disguise, really," she finished. " I might have stayed down there for years and years, never getting anywhere."

" And you want to get somewhere ? "

" To the top," Ann said frankly. " It's always been my ambition."

" Well, if you keep on as you're going, I think you've the right to hope. Now, just let us see what you can do for a few more weeks, and, if your work is up to par, we'll think about putting you on salary. Would you like that ? "

Too overwhelmed to speak, Ann could only nod her head. Then, as the editor half rose from his chair, smiling at her, she realized she was dismissed and took a blushing departure.

" Oh," she thought, as she stood for a minute outside his door, trying to regain her composure. " He's ripping ! He's simply grand. Oh, I will work hard, I will, I *will* ! "

By which it may be seen that hero worship can give an added impetus to ambition, for there was no doubt about it that Ann's brief encounter with the editor of the *Daily Record* had brought on an acute attack of that disease.

But after exaltation comes an inevitable reaction.

Ann found that the work she was being given to do differed in no way from that she had been offered in the past week. Small stories, unimportant snippets, some of them not even appearing in a single edition of the paper. Picture exhibitions, fashion specials, re-writes of little news items from abroad, were what fell to her lot.

" I might as well be back in Meffingham," she thought impatiently.

It was humiliating to go back to Molly each night with no further tales of scoops and front-page " splashes." Even Aunt Helen's letter of warm congratulation seemed ironic, now that there was no follow-up to her first triumph. Ann's spirits sank lower and lower, and she went about her day's routine with sulky indifference. Alan Weaver, she considered, might give her a big job just now and again, now that he knew she was capable of handling it. There were moments when she heard her fellow reporters discussing their work for the day, and her heart swelled with jealousy. She decided that she hated the assistant news editor.

But the hate evaporated when, just before lunch one morning, Weaver called her over to his desk.

" Look here, Ann," he said, " I'm going to trust you with a rather delicate job. It'll want careful handling, but I think you can do it."

" I'll do my best," she said eagerly.

" I know you will. Well, here's the set-up. The ex-Duchess of Trehelly—you remember that eccentric American woman who divorced the Duke last year ?—is said to be living in a little village in Wiltshire, a place called Marbroke. She's believed to be living like a farmer, doing all her own work —making butter, looking after the stock, and all that sort of thing. Every one thought she had returned to America, so an interview with her will be a really good story. I've arranged for a car to take you to Heston, and the *Record* aeroplane will be waiting there to fly you to the nearest point to Marbroke."

Ann caught her breath. This was the kind of assignment she had dreamed of during long, dull days at Meffingham. The office car ! Flying to a story ! Trusted to handle a difficult interview ! It was worth all the dreariness and frustration of the last few days, just to be sent on a job like this.

Alan Weaver was speaking again.

" The point is, Ann, that the facts of the story may already have leaked out, in which case you'll be up against some competition from other papers. That's why we're flying you, so that you get there first. Now, keep your eyes and ears open, and even if you can't make the old girl talk, anything relevant to the story will be printable."

" Right, Mr. Weaver. I'll do my utmost."

" Good girl. Off you go."

But when Ann, her mind in a seething turmoil, stepped into the fast, stream-lined car that waited for her outside the office, she had no idea what the story of the ex-Duchess of Trehelly was to bring into her life.

CHAPTER FIVE

A BUCKET OF WATER

NEVER in her life before had Ann been in an aeroplane. She was conscious of a slight sinking in the pit of her stomach as the small Tiger-Moth taxied across Heston aerodrome, turned up-wind and began to race over the turf. But once risen into the upper air, she was aware only of a great exhilaration, a sense of physical and mental well-being, tempered with a vivid curiosity.

" If the *Echo* crowd could see me now ! " she thought, hugging a mental vision of herself, Ann Thorne, of the *Record*, flying across country to do a difficult story. It was almost too good to believe !

She craned her neck to look through the tiny cabin window at the ground beneath, at the toy houses, the river that was like the silvery track of a snail, the miniature horses and cattle in fields that looked like a microscopic chess-board. The sky was a cold, uniform grey, cloudless but without warmth, and the whole world beneath and above the rocking wings of the 'plane, seemed drained of colour. Nothing appeared living or moving but the little aeroplane, zooming steadily towards a distant horizon, lifting and falling as it encountered air pockets or sudden strata of increased density.

Presently the machine began to lose altitude, banking and turning, always dropping, over a square patch of green, at one side of which was a long, narrow building. Ann could see a little group of figures, their faces turned upwards, standing beside a hangar.

The 'plane swooped down, landed up-wind with a slight bump, and jolted its way across the flying-field to a small patch of tarmac.

" Here we are," said the pilot cheerily, speaking for the first time. He opened the cabin door, and Ann climbed down, to be met immediately by a man in a chauffeur's cap.

" You the young lady from the *Record*? Right. I've got a car here, and we'd better be going. Seen a couple of chaps making for Marbroke by road in a hurry, and they may be reporters. I got my instructions to get you there with no time lost."

Ann was full of admiration for the smooth and efficient way the *Record* managed its affairs. Every detail was worked out with machine-like precision. Some day, she thought, her lips quirking with sudden humour, reporters might be obsolete, and the whole business of producing a paper done by robots operating machinery. A robot reporter barking questions and taking down the answers on a gramophone disc would be enough to frighten anybody into talking.

Now they were speeding through country lanes, the man at the wheel taking corners without slackening pace, the speedometer needle quivering at the sixty mark on straight stretches. And suddenly, at a hidden valley massed with fruit trees, he drew up with squealing brakes, turned in his seat, and indicated a glimpse of a red house, half hidden in foliage.

"That's where she lives," he said. "You'll probably find her feeding her pigs, or white-washing a barn. Queer old girl she is ; never met nobody like her."

"I suppose there's no doubt that she *is* the ex-Duchess of Trehelly ? " Ann asked. "I mean, how is it that nobody knew she was doing this, and why did the story suddenly break ? "

"There's no doubt on it," said the man. "Y'see, my daughter, Elsie, was in service for five years on the Trehelly estate. She knows the whole lot on 'em. Well, a week ago, she come home from the London house—Carlton House Terrace, you know—where she's bin for the last year. Just like every one else, she thought the old girl had upped and gorn to America after the divorce. And then, dashed if she didn't meet her Grace walking down to the village. Elsie she says, ' Why, good-morning, your Grace,' and the old girl says, ' You mustn't say that. My name is Mrs. Suter ; that's what it is, and I'm just a ordinary farmer woman.' But my Elsie, she's a smart one, she is, and she ain't like to forget a lady what she served all them years."

"So you or she tipped off the *Daily Record* ? " suggested Ann.

" Ay, that's what happened. Chap in your office promised to pay Elsie a decent sum if the story were true. But our Elsie—well, she's engaged to a lad on the *Wiltshire Herald*, and she went and let on to him one night when they was walking out. He got proper excited about it, and that's how it got out to the other papers."

" I see," said Ann, taking in just how much competition she could expect to face in securing the story. She climbed out of the car. " Well, I suppose I'd better go and see what I can do."

The old red farmhouse, when she approached it, seemed lifeless and deserted. A dog barked somewhere at the back, some hens clucked, and the sleepy crooning of pigeons came from the low-hanging eaves. But there was no sign of human life until she turned a corner of the encircling wall and almost walked into a stationary car, beside which two men stood in earnest conclave. Ann recognized one of them as Tom Welling, star reporter of the *Evening Gazette*. The other man had a camera, all set for quick action, dangling from his hand.

There was no one else to be seen, and Ann drew a breath of relief that she had only one paper, so far, to battle with for the story.

Before she could retreat, Welling turned and regarded her with amused eyes.

" You're Ann Thorne, aren't you ? I thought so—I've seen you about Fleet Street. Well, you might as well join the mourners. There's nothing doing. The old girl has locked herself in the house and her companion, Mrs. Brill, just sticks her head through the window and flatly denies any knowledge of the ex-Duchess. We've tried coaxing, bribery, bullying—every kind of approach, and the answer is a particularly sour lemon."

Ann's mind was working fast.

She said, " Well, I think I'll go in and see if Mrs. Brill won't talk to another woman. There's a chance, you know."

" We'll come with you," Tom Welling said instantly, but Ann shook her head.

" Don't be silly. It would only put her back up to see a whole crowd of us. Leave it to me, will you ? "

" Yes ; but, dash it," Tom Welling protested, " we have to get a story too."

" All right. I'll promise you this—whatever she says to me, I'll pass on to you."

And privately Ann determined to spin out her time at the farmhouse until it was too late for Welling to get a story for the last edition of his evening paper. That would mean she had an exclusive for the *Record*, and the *Evening Gazette* would not be able to publish anything until the following midday.

She pushed open the farmyard gate, went up a narrow, gravelled path, and came to a garden, ablaze with country flowers. The house brooded over it, quiet and still, though a feather of smoke from a squat chimney showed that somebody was at home. The front door was hidden in a deep porch, and Ann went up to it and knocked lightly. She waited a few minutes, and, when there was no response, knocked again.

This time, she heard a ground floor window open, and, stepping out of the porch, confronted a woman, who leaned over a window-sill and looked at her with suspicious eyes.

" Who are you ?   What do you want ? "

Ann's smile was full of coaxing charm ; but the woman's face showed no softening.   She wore an old gardening overall and a tattered straw hat, and her glance was very cold and direct.

" Mrs. Brill ? " Ann asked.   " I wonder if Mrs. Suter could spare me a few minutes to discuss something of importance ? "

" Are you a reporter ? "

For a moment Ann hesitated, unsure of what ethics dictated in such a situation.   Then she decided on complete honesty and nodded her head.

" Yes ; I'm Ann Thorne, of the *Daily Record.* Do listen to me, just for a minute, Mrs. Brill.   You see, the Press is aware that Mrs. Suter is actually the ex-Duchess of Trehelly, and until some one gets the full story of her life here at the farm, you are liable to be pestered with reporters."

" We *are* pestered," Mrs. Brill remarked grimly.

" Exactly.   But don't you see that if her Grace will give just one interview, the other papers will lose interest and you'll be left in peace ?   If you can persuade her to give me a ten-minute talk I can

promise you that'll be the last you'll hear of any
of us."

Mrs. Brill looked thoughtful.

" I appreciate your point, but I don't think I
can do much. Mrs. Suter hates reporters. Her
orders are that she will see nobody."

" But if you put forward what I've just suggested. . . ."

In her eagerness, seeing the first signs of capitula-
tion, Ann went nearer to the window, looking at Mrs.
Brill with sparkling eyes.

" Will you just ask her, Mrs. Brill ? "

" Well. . . ."

At that moment a window above opened with a
clatter and a bucket of ice-cold water descended on
Ann's head. It was a large bucketful, and she was
drenched to the skin.

A voice from over her head cried, " Get off my
property and stay off it ! I've got a shotgun here,
and I know how to use it."

Gasping, spluttering, chilled to the bone, Ann
looked up into the malevolent eyes of the ex-Duchess
of Trehelly.

" Go on," shouted that lady, her voice edged
with exasperation. " Get off my land ! You're
trespassing, in any case, or perhaps you Paul Prys
don't know or care about such things ? Go on,
get out ! "

" You'd better go," said Mrs. Brill.

Ann looked up again.

" You're very silly," she said severely. " Don't

you realize you've given me a much better story than any interview I could publish ? "

But the ex-Duchess of Trehelly was beside herself with anger.

" Publish and be hanged ! " she shouted. " But you'd better warn any other reporters who think I'm a ' story ' that they'll be met with worse than water. And I mean what I say."

" I'll forget the water if you'll come down and talk to me," Ann offered mildly, still fighting hard for the real story her paper wanted. " Please. . . ."

But the window closed with a slam, and Mrs. Brill, laughing now, said, " She'll use that gun if she feels like it. You'd better be on your way, Miss Thorne."

" Right," Ann said crisply. She turned away and went back through the garden to the farmhouse gate.

Tom Welling and the camera-man regarded her with incredulous eyes. Water dripped from the edge of her hat, from the hem and sleeves of her heavy tweed coat, from her eyelashes, chin, and even from the fingertips of her gloves.

" What did you do ? Fall in the pond ? "

" Yes," Ann said firmly. " I tripped on something. Well, I'm going back to town. You were quite right—there's nothing doing, nothing at all. I give you my word of honour I didn't get an interview."

Welling shrugged hopelessly and moved towards his car.

" Well, that's that, I suppose. I shall come back again to-morrow, though. Can't let a good story like this die on us."

Ann, thinking of the shotgun threat, stifled a giggle. If Welling really meant to try again, perhaps she ought to warn him, but, if she mentioned it, he would assume at once that she had actually talked to the ex-Duchess. Better say nothing. After all, she doubted if even that angry lady would direct a gun deliberately at another human being.

Climbing back into the car, she thought, " I've never had such an exciting time in all my life. Oh, just wait until Alan Weaver hears about it ! "

It was cold in the little cabin of the aeroplane and shivers began to chase each other beneath Ann's skin. Her sodden clothes hung heavily about her slender body, and her feet, in their light shoes, felt like small blocks of ice. Before they landed at Heston she had sneezed half a dozen times.

" Dash it," she thought crossly. " Now I've caught a cold. It's these wet clothes. But I must go to the office and knock out my story before I can go home and change."

Her colleagues in the *Record* news room regarded her with astounded eyes, but Ann had no time to explain her bedraggled condition. She went straight to Alan Weaver's desk.

" Mr. Weaver, I saw the ex-Duchess of Trehelly, but she wouldn't give me an interview. She threw a bucket of water over me instead. Is that a story ? "

" *Is* it ? Here, come along and see Phillips."

Without ceremony, she was hustled into the presence of Gregory Phillips and made to tell her story in detail.

" You look a bit knocked up," Phillips said, looking at her anxiously. " Do you feel up to writing the whole thing for us ? You can go home to bed then."

" Of course," said Ann stoutly. " I'll be all right."

But it was difficult, writing that story. Her head felt muzzy and once or twice the whole great room seemed to swim round her. But she banged away obstinately on a typewriter, and finally carried the completed sheets to Weaver. He looked up at her, noted the flushed and burning face, the overbright eyes, and gave an exclamation of alarm.

" I'm going to send some one home with you in a taxi," he said abruptly. " You ought to be in bed, with some one to look after you. Don't come in to-morrow if you feel rotten."

" I—I shall be quite well—to-morrow," said Ann faintly. A great shudder went through her frame and she swayed.

She never knew that it was Roger Blaydon's arm that went round her, Roger Blaydon who guided her faltering steps to the lift, where a sympathetic Pugs shot them downwards and dashed out into the street for a taxi. By now there was a pounding in her ears, and a sharp, nagging pain behind her shoulder-blades, a pain that was aggravated every time she drew a breath. The whole world was like a strange, distorted dream, in which people moved and spoke, becoming at one moment gigantic, wavering figures, shrinking away, at the next, into pigmy forms. And she was very, very tired. . . .

The dream went on interminably. Sometimes she was struggling, with a new and vicious cunning, against a rival reporter for a story about a European war, a secret war, about whom nobody knew except herself and her rival. Sometimes she was desperately trying to type an important article, with a crowd of waiting sub-editors pressing about her. But every time she came to the end of a page, it was to find the sheet quite blank, and she had to begin again. Once she cried out " It isn't my fault—oh, it isn't my fault ! " and some one with a voice like Aunt Helen's said, " Of course it isn't, darling. Go to sleep, like a good girl."

She would have liked to sleep, but the pain under her shoulder-blades stabbed at her, and her chest felt as if it must burst in her effort to get some air down to her tortured lungs. The pillow—she had no idea how she came to have a pillow—burned her cheeks, and the coverings over her weighed on her limbs with a dead weight. . . .

And then, one morning, the dream faded away and she opened dazed eyes to find herself in a strange room, a narrow white room, with ranked vases of flowers splashing colour from an austere dressing-chest. And by her side stood Aunt Helen, smiling at her, holding her hand in a firm and comforting clasp.

"Aunt . . . Helen ? " Ann's voice was a whisper. "What . . .? Why . . .?"

"Don't talk, darling. You've been ill, but you'll soon be well again now."

A nurse in a snowy cap and apron came to the other side of the bed and proffered a feeding-cup.

"Drink this, and then go straight off to sleep again," she said.

Ann sipped at the beef-tea, her eyes roving wonderingly about the room, coming back to Aunt Helen's face with a puzzled stare. And suddenly, at a thought that flashed through her mind, she made an effort to sit up.

"My job, Aunt Helen ? My job . . . have I lost it ? "

Aunt Helen pushed her gently back on the pillow.

"On the contrary. You seem to be the office heroine. There's a letter for you from the editor, and I'll read it to you after you've had some sleep."

"No, now," said Ann's hoarse, exhausted voice. "Read it now, Aunt Helen. I couldn't sleep until I know."

"Very well, dear. I'll go and get it."

But when Aunt Helen came back, the letter in her hand, it was to find Ann fast asleep, breathing lightly and peacefully, her hands, lying on the coverlet, cool and dry for the first time for weeks.

It was dusk when she awoke, but Aunt Helen was still there, and the first thought in Ann's mind was for her letter. Switching on a shaded bedlight, Aunt Helen read it to her.

Because Ann had sustained her illness in the cause of duty, wrote John Grimthorpe, the *Daily Record* office would, of course, deal with all expenses that her illness incurred. And Ann, herself, had been placed on the salary list since the first pay-day after the ex-Duchess of Trehelly episode. At ten guineas a week.

" That's three weeks ago," Aunt Helen said.

" Have I been ill for three weeks ? " demanded Ann huskily.

" Yes, darling, just over. You just escaped double-pneumonia. You gave me an awful fright," said poor Aunt Helen, breaking suddenly into the tears she hadn't shed once since Roger Blaydon had telegraphed her to come to London.

" Oh, darling," said Ann remorsefully. " Please don't cry. I'll be up and whizzing about again in no time, you'll see. This letter is like a trip round the world to me. I can't wait to get back to the office."

" Don't talk so much, dear. You mustn't get tired. Don't you want to know where all the flowers came from ? "

Ann's head nodded wearily. Yes ; she was tired, but so happily and pleasantly tired, with the weariness that comes after a long country walk, or some more intense physical effort.

" They're from all your friends at the *Record*. One or another of them has called every day, and that big pot of roses comes from the editor personally."

Ann lay in her narrow bed, weak as a baby, but thrilling with happiness. She had made good! She was accepted! Why, it even seemed that she had gained affection among her colleagues. Life was wonderful. It was kind and generous and understanding to those who did their best—and that she had done her best, Ann knew. She determined now to get strong as fast as possible, to get out of the nursing home to which she had been taken, to get back to her hostel and her job without any more delay.

She thought, with a sudden, surprising chuckle, " If that old Duchess person knew what she'd done for me, wouldn't she be furious? " And on the heels of that thought came another.

" Aunt Helen. Please may I see my story about the ex-Duchess of Trehelly? Did you cut it for me? "

" Yes, dear. I've got it here, among your letters and papers. Here it is."

She spread in front of Ann the front page of the *Daily Record*, dated three weeks back.

DUCHESS THROWS WATER OVER *DAILY RECORD* REPORTER

said the headlines, stretching over four columns of type. There were sub-heads that cried, " Farmhouse Scene. Divorced wife of Lord Trehelly found farming in Wiltshire. She is not in America. And she hates reporters."

And just above the story proper, in capitals that actually caught the eye, were the magic, unbelievable words

By ANN THORNE.

Ann caught her breath, and suddenly tears rushed to her eyes. She looked at Aunt Helen and faltered, " They—they've *signed my story!* Oh, did you see it, darling ? They've signed my story."

" Yes," said Aunt Helen, smiling. " I saw it. I want to say now, my dearest Ann, that you were right all along. You *are* a born newspaper-woman, and I'll never object to it again. I didn't realize that wanting to be a journalist is as important as wanting to be a musician, or an artist, or anything creative. Bless you, darling, and congratulations with all my heart."

She stooped to kiss Ann, and Ann's arms went weakly about her neck.

" Darling Aunt Helen. . . ."

Two weeks later, Ann walked back into the offices of the *Daily Record.* From the moment she pushed open the swing door from the street it seemed that everybody had a word and a smile for her. The commissionaire came hurrying to her side, put an arm under her elbow as she mounted the few steps to the lift, and kept his finger on the bell with ferocious determination.

" Glad to see you back, Miss Thorne. Quite better now, I hope ? "

" Quite, thank you, Roberts."

Little Pugs almost bowed to the ground.

" Step in, Miss Thorne. Hope you're better, Miss ? Sorry to keep you waiting, Miss."

And in the news room her colleagues clustered round her.

" Hallo there, Ann. Are you better ? " " Nice to see you, Ann. Come and have some tea, this afternoon ? " " Oh, look, Ann Thorne's back. Hallo, Ann ! Feeling okay ? "

Ann was certainly feeling okay. Her heart was warm with friendliness and gratitude, and tears pressed behind her eyes and throat ; she could never express to those around her how much she appreciated their interest and sympathy. Before she was ill she had been just another reporter, no one of any great moment. But now she had become, suddenly and delightfully, a personality in the office. Smiling and a little shy she stood among her friends and assured them that she was quite well again and glad to be back.

Roger Blaydon said, " You're awfully thin, Ann."

" Well," laughed Ann, " that's better than being awfully fat ! "

Alan Weaver's smile was kindly.

" We've missed you, Ann. Now I want you to pop down into the East End and call at this address. The man there claims he has the cleverest trained parrot in the world. Apparently it can do anything but make clothes. Take a camera-man, will you ? "

She was back in harness again and it felt grand.

For the next few days she was given only easy stories to do, jobs that Weaver evidently picked with the object of saving her strength and energy. But as time passed more important stories came her way, and by the end of a few months she had seen her name over her work no fewer than eight times.

She no longer lived at the Baker Street hostel. Ten guineas a week meant that she could afford a tiny flat, and she had taken one in a block off Chancery Lane and was sharing it with Molly Andrews. The two girls enjoyed housekeeping together, and vied with each other at cooking experiments and labour-saving ideas. Every now and again they would give a party, to which Ann would invite Roger Blaydon and Marta Raines and one or two other reporters, while Molly's guests were fellow clerks from her office.

Life was full and very good to Ann in those days. She could own to a good working knowledge of London, and even the remoter parts of Britain were no longer mysteries to her ; she was sent to Scotland, Wales, the Midlands, even once to Ireland. She had been to Paris to attend the wedding of a Balkan princess, and to Holland to interview a young millionairess who was building a home there.

In fact, she thought sometimes, reviewing her day's activities, a dream had come true. Every week she sent a pound home to Aunt Helen to save for her, and sometimes she was able to dash down to Harfold for twenty-four hours. She revelled then in the green peace of the country, in the quiet nights, and the long talks with her beloved aunt. But she was always anxious, in the morning, to get back again to Fleet Street, to find out what work had been scheduled for her, to strain mind and nerve in an effort to get yet another front page story to her credit.

Once, while she was cycling through Meffingham, she met Bill Morgan. His hat was still at its jaunty angle, but she thought he looked sad and dispirited.

" You're quite a big shot these days, aren't you ? " he asked her.

" Oh, I don't know," Ann said diffidently. " I've had a lot of luck."

" Luck," mused Bill. " Yes, I suppose luck has something to do with it. I don't seem to have any. I suppose you couldn't put in a word for me with your news editor ? "

" I could, Bill, but I don't know if it would do any good. I will, if you like."

" Will you, Ann ? That would be ripping of you. Let me know what he says, will you ? "

And Ann, remembering a promise of exactly the same sort that had been made to her nearly a year ago, resolved to speak to Gregory Phillips, and write at once to Bill Morgan, telling him the result.

She kept her word and talked to Gregory Phillips about her ex-colleague on the *Evening Echo*.

" Tell him to come and see me," Phillips said briefly. " If he's any good at all I daresay we could find a corner for him."

So that it was without surprise one morning that Ann walked into the office and saw Bill Morgan grinning at her from an obscure corner desk.

"It's all due to you," he said presently, his eyes full of gratitude. "I'm only on space, but I expect I can make more than I did in Meffingham, and anyway, I've got to Fleet Street."

"Good luck, Bill. I hope you make a grand success of it."

It was about this time that Ann, going to interview a young society girl who was rumoured to be a secret mannequin at a large fashion house, found herself drawn into a party of gay young people. They were attractive, wealthy, irresponsible, and seemed to take a great liking to Ann. She was deluged with invitations to luncheons and dinners, to bathing parties on the river, to Hurlingham and Ranelagh.

The girl she had gone to interview, pretty young Corinne West, youngest daughter of the Earl of Axe, found in Ann a new experience, a new toy, something to be examined, and, if possible, exploited. And Ann, flattered by this attention, was only too eager to spend all her spare time with her new friend.

"You're never at home in the evening now," Molly complained more than once. "You don't come in till all hours, and you're beginning to look frightfully pulled-down and tired. I'm sure they'll begin to notice it in your office soon. And besides, it's lonely without you."

"Oh, Molly, don't fuss," Ann would say impatiently. "I'm having a marvellous time. And what if the office does notice ? I'm doing my work, aren't I ? "

"I don't know," answered Molly, looking thoughtful. "It doesn't seem to have the sparkle it used to. It seems sort of mechanical. And you haven't had a signed special for ages."

"Well, what of it ? You can't build your whole life around your work."

"You *used* to," Molly said.

It was true that Ann's work was losing some of its freshness. She was still thrilled to be Ann Thorne, of the *Daily Record*, but now, it seemed, the thrill was merely for *being* and not for *doing*. She scamped her stories, eager to be out and away with Corinne and her crowd. Twice in a month she made a hash of a biggish story, for the sole reason that she was so tired after a succession of late nights that she missed something essential said to her.

At last came a morning when she was told to go to Staines to talk to a man who had been a General in the war, and was now living in the infirmary. But that day Corinne had planned to take her whole crowd to a special matinée at which an American comedian, visiting London, was to appear for the first and only time. And Ann wanted to go to that matinée.

She went to it. She appeared again in the office about six and told Alan Weaver that the man at Staines couldn't see her until the next day, that he was not well enough to be interviewed.

" Well, go to-morrow, will you ? " Weaver said casually, and Ann had the grace to feel ashamed of herself in the face of such trust.

The next day nearly all the important papers carried an interview with the destitute General, for the Staines journalist who had found it, disappointed that the *Daily Record* reporter had failed to show up, telephoned the other papers and gave the story away.

Gregory Phillips sent for Ann.

" Look here, young woman," he said, without preliminaries. " You've been working for us for a year. During ten months of that time your work has been good, but for the last two months it's been frankly bad. What's the matter ? Have you anything on your mind ? "

Ann fought the temptation to lie, to say her aunt was ill, to wriggle somehow out of the lecture she knew was coming to her. But her essential honesty won, and she said, " No, Mr. Phillips. Nothing at all."

" Then why this slackness ? Why these missed stories ? I don't understand you, I must say. We took a chance on you, when no other paper I can think of would give work to a seventeen-year-old girl, and we gave you the opportunity to make good. What other girl do you know who's in the position to earn ten guineas a week at seventeen ? Why are you letting us down ? "

Shamed colour rushed up over Ann's cheeks. It was quite true, she *had* been letting her paper down. She remembered how good all the staff had been to her when she was ill. Every one had been kind to her. They had trusted her, and she had betrayed their trust.

Tears welled up into her eyes and brimmed over as she said, " I've been a fool, Mr. Phillips. I—I made friends with Corinne West—and I—I——"

" *That* bunch of young good-for-nothings ! " said Gregory Phillips in contempt.

Ann said, " I'm sorry now. They seemed such fun—more fun than anything else. I'm sorry, truly I am, Mr. Phillips. Will you give me another chance ? I won't let you down again."

" I hope you won't. Jobs aren't easy to find in this street, and they aren't easy to hold. We wouldn't like to let you go, Ann, but efficiency and accuracy are our watchwords here, and every one of the staff, from the highest to the lowest, is expected to remember that."

The tears came in earnest now.

" I *will* remember. I'm most terribly sorry, and I won't let it happen again."

" Very well, then. Run along and be a good girl."

It wasn't easy to shake off Corinne West and her friends. They rang up the office constantly. They called at the Chancery Lane flat, demanding that Ann should go out with them to this or that festivity. Corinne West didn't like being robbed of her new toy until she was tired of it, and Ann's refusal to be one of her band of admirers made her keener than ever to have the young reporter in her company.

Sometimes Ann would be persuaded into going